The Tales of Fluke & Tash

Egyptian Adventure

Fluke and Tash series:

Robin Hood Adventure

Egyptian Adventure

The Tales of Fluke & Tash

Egyptian Adventure

MARK ELVY

Available from

www.ypdbooks.com

and

www.flukeandtash.com

Published by Fluke & Tash Publishing

A CIP catalogue record for this book is available from the British Library.

ISBN 978-0-9934956-3-2

Book layout by Clare Brayshaw

Prepared and printed by:

York Publishing Services Ltd
64 Hallfield Road
Layerthorpe
York YO31 7ZQ

Tel: 01904 431213

Website: www.yps-publishing.co.uk

1274BC

Fly like the wind...

The troubled looking figure was pacing up and down, deep in thought. Ramesses II had walked around the perimeter of his extremely large tent, up and down the middle, and back around the perimeter in the opposite direction. It didn't matter which route he took, he still ended up in the same place and unfortunately with the same answer. He'd been too hasty, that was now obvious. It was one of his few minor flaws. Impatience was a family trait, maybe even a slight weakness. Not one of his trusty aides had dared to question their beloved Pharaoh, well except one, Addaya. He had questioned Ramesses before he left. So much so they had an argument the day before his army had departed the city of Pi-Ramesses on their long march north.

Addaya, if only you were here now my friend he thought to himself. Well his impatience could lead him and his overstretched army headlong into trouble. He knew Addaya and the reinforcements were at least a month's hard march behind. His other three regiments were closer but still some way off.

His thoughts were interrupted by the entrance of one of his generals. Coughing politely before he entered the tent, he bowed before speaking.

'My lord, the interrogation is over. It would seem we've been duped by the two captured spies. The Hittite army lead by Muwatalli is a lot closer than we were lead to believe. The bulk of their main force are camped outside the old town of Kadesh and poised to strike.'

Ramesses nodded that he understood the implications and the general retreated from the tent to leave a troubled Ramesses with his thoughts.

He reached for some parchment paper and began drafting some brief notes explaining his predicament. Satisfied with the finished letter, he ordered an aide to fetch one of his swiftest carrier pigeons. Ramesses ensured the letter was tied firmly to his finest pigeon, kissed the bird on the head and whispered *make haste and fly like the wind.*

The bird was released into the air and flew around several times, got his bearings and flew off in the direction of Pi-Ramesses. Watching the bird disappear into the distance all he could now do was pray to the gods and hope...

Present day

It's just a dream Fluke...

Fluke heard an eerie sound like no other come from somewhere behind him, *Shiiiiiiiing* closely followed by *Swiiiiiiiish* as the sword, removed from its sheath, cut through the air with ease. He ducked, and the sharp gleaming sword missed him by inches. Sparks flew as it crashed into the stone pillar just where his head had been, and bits of stone crumbled to the floor. Having ducked in time, he turned to see where the next attack would come from. The battle was raging all around him and he needed to stay alert. He went on the offensive and lunged at his attacker causing the big burly oaf to stumble backwards.

'Fluke, Fluke, Fluuuuuuke...!' He heard the voice but couldn't see who had shouted his name. His body began to shake uncontrollably. He felt paws on his shoulders shaking him.

'*Fluke, will you wake up!*' He leapt up with a start and tripped over the edge of his bed. Bleary eyed, he gazed around the room and took in his comfy bed, leather sofa, carpet and television. Not a stone pillar or attacking soldier in sight.

Tash, who was stood with her paws resting on her hips, didn't look too impressed, and realisation dawned on Fluke that he had been dreaming.

'You really do make a racket when you're snoring and dreaming you know,' said Tash.

'Dreaming? It felt ever so realistic! I was battling the Sheriff's soldiers again!' said Fluke, tongue hanging out of the side of his mouth as he acted out some intricate moves with a pretend sword causing Tash to laugh.

'Yeah not bad I suppose,' confirmed Tash admiring Fluke's pretend swordplay. 'We certainly taught the Sheriff's men a lesson, but to be fair we did have a fantastic teacher in Robin Hood,' said Tash.

'I wonder how Robin, Little John and the rest of the gang are getting on?' said Fluke, 'I know it's only been a couple of weeks since we left but I really miss them.'

'Well, we can pop back any time,' confirmed Tash, 'we've only got to dust down our magic suitcase, and Robin did say to drop in one day.'

Two weeks had passed since their first adventure together in Sherwood Forest, helping Robin Hood and his band of merry men battle the evil Sheriff of Nottingham, rescue Robin's beloved Maid Marion from the castle fortress and be best men at their wedding.

Phew, what an adventure that had been! Sword fights; archery competitions; making weapons; tree houses; a daring rescue mission and learning to play medieval musical instruments. That was Fluke's first adventure, and Tash, the seasoned traveller who had been on many adventures on her own, was now glad to have a travelling companion and had promised Fluke many more adventures using their special secret – the magic, time travelling suitcase.

'About that magic suitcase...' said Fluke, 'where are we going next? Mum and Dad are out at work, we've got the house to ourselves, a magic suitcase upstairs just begging to be used again, c'mon Tash let's go on another adventure!'

'We will Fluke, just got to finalise some plans and then Egypt here we come!'

'So we're definitely off to Egypt then?'

'Well, you saw that Egyptian documentary on television and said you wanted some sun, sand and water, Fluke! We'll go to the Valley of the Kings, see some pyramids and take a boat trip down the River Nile.'

'So what are we waiting for? Let's go!' said an eager Fluke.

'We've got a meeting lined up with the Nummers later this morning, they're a fountain of knowledge and it might be an idea to speak to them, and see if they can give us some advice on ancient Egypt before we go.'

It was agreed; the Nummers had been around for centuries, so their ancient ancestors would have surely lived in Egypt. Later that morning they would meet with the Nummers outside their tree stump in the back garden and see what they could learn about Egypt and Pharaohs before they set off on their next adventure.

Egyptian Nummers...

Fluke and Tash met outside and stood patiently by the old tree stump. Tash had used her cat flap as normal and Fluke had now got used to unlocking the patio door by himself, using his secret key they'd had cut, so that he could let himself in and out whenever he pleased.

Fluke used his paw and gently tapped on the tiny hidden door at the base of the tree stump. They waited patiently until the door opened, and out strode the small family of Nummers, beaming from ear to ear as they were always pleased to see Fluke and Tash whom they regarded as close friends.

'So Tash tells us you're both off again on another adventure?' said Pappa Nummer.

'We certainly are,' confirmed Fluke, eager to get started and be on their way to Egypt. 'So what can you tell us about Egypt? Any information and advice would be great,' he continued.

'Depends...' said Pappa Nummer, 'what sort of adventures are you looking for? I mean Egypt has been around for thousands of years. It's seen many Pharaohs, has a lot of history, and was a hugely powerful nation.'

Fluke looked at Tash, scratched an itchy spot behind his ear and said 'Dunno really, your ancestors were around then, what would you suggest?'

Pappa Nummer turned to his wife and they both said together, 'Ramesses II would be a great choice.'

'Ramesses II?' said Tash. 'Yes, now you come to mention it I have heard the name before.'

'He is widely considered the greatest Pharaoh of all time...' continued Pappa Nummer, really getting into his stride now. 'He had a long and successful life, lived until he was 90 years old and reigned for about 66 years, building huge cities, magnificent temples and monuments, quite extraordinary really, in fact a lot of our relatives were expert stonemasons helping build his pyramids and temples so you might even meet some of our ancestors.'

'Cool!' said Fluke hanging onto every word that Pappa Nummer told them. 'What about chariot racing?' Fluke asked, 'I've always fancied having a go in one of those!'

Pappa Nummer reached inside his front door and brought out an ancient looking scroll, rolled up and tied with a red ribbon. Undoing the knot, he carefully opened the manuscript and laid it gently on the ground. Fluke and Tash gathered round to see what was written down.

It was a Nummer family tree, dating back centuries with notes added alongside each date. Tash ran her paw down the list and made a decision, '1274BC...' she looked at Fluke, paw hovering over the date mentioned, 'Ramesses II versus the Hittite Empire, the biggest chariot battle ever fought. You said you wanted chariots Fluke, well you'll get to see plenty of them here!'

The conversations went on a while longer, and discussions went back and forth with both Fluke and Tash asking as many questions as they could think of. They were both sure there were hundreds more they could have asked but didn't have the time.

It was decided, a unanimous decision by everybody, the date agreed was 1274BC, ancient Egypt. Fluke was excited and couldn't wait.

'Are we going to leave tonight Tash?' he said excitedly, 'because if we are, I better go and start packing a few things to take with us.'

Tash turned to the Nummers and thanked them for their help and the use of their ancient scroll, when Pappa Nummer said, 'If you manage to bump into any of our relatives say hello for us, and tell them the Nummer family line is still as strong as ever in their future.'

Will he never go to sleep...?

As Fluke locked up the patio door and stored his secret key inside his collar, they both heard Dad's car coming down the street. Mum and Dad were back from work and ready for a night in front of the television.

'Crickey, we've been in the garden a while.' Tash turned to Fluke, 'You really can chatter when you get going,' she said.

'I can't help it Tash, the Nummers are so interesting to talk to,' said Fluke, as the pair made their way up the stairs, onto the landing, under the ironing board and headed for their bedroom and the comfy sofa, and assumed their standard positions – Fluke one end and Tash the other, curled up as if they had been there all day.

The evening went by slowly. Dinner was cooked by Mum, whilst Dad served up Fluke and Tash's food. Fluke devoured his in seconds. Tash, as normal, nibbled daintily at her small bowl of fish, and the rest of the evening was spent with Fluke and Tash curled up by the fire pretending to watch the television, secretly looking at the cuckoo clock on the wall, willing the time to reach bedtime, hoping that Mum and Dad didn't find an interesting late night film to watch.

Eleven o'clock came round and thankfully Dad started yawning which woke up Mum who had fallen asleep midway through a drama that she had mentioned earlier: *Ooh we must watch that later...* but had missed most of the show.

Dad made Fluke pop out to the garden for his night time toilet break, then with a ruffle of Tash and Fluke's heads, bid them both good night. 'See you two in the morning and behave yourselves,' he said, flicking off the light switch, leaving the pair in near total darkness. The only visible light was from the street lamps outside which attempted to penetrate the curtains and the faint glow from the remaining log on the fire.

'Give it half an hour, Fluke,' Tash whispered, 'you know Dad always reads his book before bedtime,' and the pair settled back down in front of the fireside, both appreciating the residual heat emanating from the dying embers that had been left to burn out, the fire guard doing its job.

Half an hour came and went, and Fluke looked expectantly at Tash trying to gauge her expression in the near darkness.

'C'mon Tash, can we go yet?' Fluke asked impatiently.

'Not yet Fluke, just wait a bit longer.'

'Well he's taking his time, won't he ever go to sleep?'

Another 20 minutes passed when they both heard the now familiar snoring coming from Mum and Dad's bedroom.

'At last,' whispered Tash, 'he's asleep now, took longer than normal, it must be a good book!'

Fluke leapt up and gingerly made his way after Tash who had started the long climb up the stairs, both heading towards the spare room, where their magic suitcase was waiting in the wardrobe.

Fancy dress...

The wardrobe door was opened by a very eager Fluke, desperate to start a new adventure, and had taken to time travel as if it was the most natural thing in the world.

Reaching into the far recess of the wardrobe, they located the magic suitcase, dragged it out onto the bedroom floor and there it lay, a very unassuming looking case it had to be said; battered and covered in scratches, held together by bits of tape, it certainly had seen better days.

'You sure you are ready for this Fluke?' said Tash.

'C'mon Tash let's get our costumes on and get going,' Fluke urged.

Tash flicked open the latch causing the case lid to spring open and studied the old book containing all the co-ordinates and date settings, then carefully used the combination lock dials on the case to set the right co-ordinates.

Tash reached into the zip compartment, felt some items of clothing and pulled out her costume.

Fluke reached in afterwards and pulled out a similar looking costume. 'It amazes me this case,' he said shaking his head, 'clever how it picks the right costume for the right date.'

'That's why it's magic Fluke,' Tash grinned, 'you wouldn't get a case like this from any shop uptown, this one's unique and it's all ours!'

Costumes were rapidly thrown on and whilst Tash's fitted perfectly, Fluke's was loose and baggy and needed a belt tied at the waist. He stood and studied himself in the full length mirror located in the wardrobe door.

'It's a miniskirt!' he said in horror, 'everybody will laugh at me! Skirts are meant to be for girls!'

Tash sniggered and tried, unsuccessfully, to hide her laughter behind her paw.

'No Fluke,' she giggled again, 'it's not a skirt, it's called a shendyt, all the men wore them, it's made of linen and will keep you cool in the subtropical heat.'

Fluke was still unsure and kept looking at his reflection in the mirror.

'Well it still looks like a skirt to me! If mine's called a shendyt, then what's yours called?'

'Kalasiris,' Tash said studying herself in the mirror. 'It's a bit longer than your miniskirt,' she joked, 'look, a full length number which sits just above the ankle.' She did a slow 360 degree turn and admired herself from all angles.

To complete the outfit, Tash reached into the case one more time and retrieved an assortment of earrings, bracelets, necklaces and some sandals to put on their paws.

'Here, put some of these on.' She handed Fluke a necklace and bracelet, 'It will finish off the costume nicely and the sandals will come in handy.'

'Thanks Tash,' Fluke muttered as he busied himself with the jewellery and bangles provided by Tash, 'you can keep the sandals though, I think I'll opt for the barefoot look as it's more trendy!'

'You'll need the sandals Fluke, trust me,' said a concerned Tash, but Fluke was adamant that he was going barefoot and put the sandals back in the case.

The pair had one final appraisal of their outfits in the mirror and concluded they couldn't get a more authentic look, shut the wardrobe door and headed over to the waiting case.

Sore paws...

Tash stood beside the magic case and waited patiently for Fluke, whose head was under the bed as he tried to retrieve something. He dragged out a bucket and spade and made his way over to the magic suitcase.

'Fluke, why have you got a bucket and spade?' said Tash, a hint of impatience in her voice.

Fluke looked sheepishly at Tash.

'The seaside Tash! You said we're going to see some sun, sand and water so I thought we could build some sand castles!'

'Put them in the case then Fluke but I really don't think we will have time to build sand castles – if all goes according to plan we'll be building pyramids, not sand castles!'

They both sat astride the magic suitcase, Tash double checked the co-ordinates one last time and Fluke glanced over at the digital clock and noted the time of 12:22, the same departure time as their last adventure.

Tash turned the handle on the case three times, which seems to engage the gears, the room started to spin and the wind picked up.

'Yeeehaaaaaa, we're off!' shouted Fluke above the noise of the wind, his ears flapping, and yet again he couldn't resist a quick peek down over the edge of the magic suitcase. Lots of fluffy white clouds below that looked like a large white rug had replaced the original beige carpet in the spare room.

'I must stop doing that,' he muttered to himself with his eyes now firmly shut. He really didn't like heights too much.

Seconds later Fluke noticed a real change in temperature. What had been a slightly chilly evening back home had now turned into a heatwave. He opened his eyes to be dazzled by the glaring sunshine and noticed mile upon mile of sand, it certainly seemed to be the biggest beach in the world. Undulating sand dunes were evident as far as the eye could see. Dotted here and there amongst the dunes were very impressive looking stone temples and pyramids but the most impressive sight was the mighty River Nile, which looked like a huge long serpent, snaking its way through the very heart of Egypt.

The magic suitcase skidded to a halt against the base of a stone structure, throwing up a mini sandstorm that covered the pair from head to paw in sand. Tash brushed herself down and gazed up, and up, and up, straining her neck to see the top.

'Wow!' she breathed, 'it's enormous!'

'Certainly is,' said Fluke in complete awe, craning his neck to see the very top. 'Nice landing by the way. You've certainly got better since our last trip, and if you keep improving like that you can throw away your L-plates!' he joked.

The pair climbed off the case and Tash stood admiring their surroundings, with one of her paws covering her eyes as the sunlight was very bright, making her squint.

'Should have brought some sunglasses,' she muttered as she busied herself making sure the case was locked. Tash was getting ready to head off towards the local village nestled near the banks of the Nile that she had spotted during the landing, when she glanced over at Fluke who was hopping from one paw to another, performing what looked like some sort of ancient Egyptian tribal dance, blowing on his paws to try and cool them down.

'Hot, hot, hot!' he said breathlessly, 'the sand is *soooo hot*!' he said in some distress as he was obviously in a fair amount of pain.

'Told you the sandals would come in handy, Fluke,' laughed Tash, who retrieved Fluke's sandals from the case and watched as he rapidly slipped his paws inside, the relief evident on his face now his paws weren't being burnt by the blazing hot sand. 'Give it a couple of days to get used to the heat and then we can both go barefoot, you're used to nice comfy carpets Fluke, and soft green grass, not scorching hot sand.'

Bastet, Cat Goddess...

They headed off towards the village, and this time it was Fluke's turn to drag the case.

'Oh, I notice it's my turn with the case when we have to hike miles,' he grumbled sarcastically to Tash, who was oblivious to his moaning. 'Why can't we just hide it back there in the sand?' he continued and then looked up in envy, because in the distance he spied a camel train, a long line of slow moving camels, fully laden with passengers and luggage of all different shapes and sizes transporting their owners away from the village they were heading for.

'Are you for real Fluke?' Tash stopped and stared at the moaning Fluke. 'So how do you think we'd ever find it again out here in this sand? It all looks the same, sand dune after sand dune. If we lose it out here we'll be stranded in Egypt for ever! We need to find a safe place to hide it in the village, so stop whining, keep up and follow me!'

'Can't we hire a camel taxi like those guys over there?' he pointed to the distant camel train disappearing over a rather large sand dune. 'It would certainly make life a lot easier.' He puffed and panted as he made his way up a small dune, his sandals trying to dig into the sand and stop himself slipping back to the bottom.

'No Fluke, not yet anyway, maybe we'll have a ride on one later, but first we've got to get to the village,' and with that she strode off, leaving Fluke to struggle on with the case. Looking over her shoulder she heard muttering noises.

'And no camel jokes either,' she pleaded, 'I know what you're thinking, and the jokes won't be funny!'

'I wasn't going to tell any camel jokes,' said Fluke defensively, 'but now you come to mention it Tash, those camels do look like they've got the *hump* having to carry so much luggage about,' he chuckled to himself. Now in full flow he continued. 'Why don't camels walk any faster? Because there's too many speed *humps* around...' he smirked. 'Or what do you call a camel without any humps? *Hump-free*!' and the jokes flowed, Fluke's sense of humour had returned with a vengeance, his struggle with the case now forgotten as he entertained himself.

Before long they had traversed the steep slope of the sand dune, reached the summit and were heading down, slipping and sliding a bit, but thankfully the slope levelled out and a straight path lay ahead, taking them directly towards the village.

The steady flow of camel hump jokes slowly dried up, much to the relief of Tash, and as they walked side by side on the smooth sandy track, they noticed a figure walking towards them. As they got closer, Tash whispered to Fluke: *'Male teenager, looks to be about 14 and is dressed just like you Fluke, so you've no worries about your costume looking out of place.'*

'Phew, that's a relief, I must admit I was a bit unsure,' he whispered back out of the corner of his mouth.

As they got closer to each other, Fluke could see that the teenage boy had his arms full. He was carrying what looked like rolls of parchment paper, similar to the Nummers family tree scroll, which were stacked so high that the boy could hardly see where he was going. He also carried what appeared to be a small wooden palette, a set of brushes and some funny looking pens.

The boy stared at Tash and as they passed he bowed in reverence, holding the position until Fluke and Tash had completely walked by. Unfortunately, the armful of parchment rolls, brushes and pens he was clutching dropped unceremoniously into a heap on the floor.

Tash stopped, turned, and bent down to help the young lad pick up his papers, as she felt obliged, as he had bowed to her and felt it was her fault the boy dropped his belongings.

'Good morning,' she said to the boy, 'my name is Tash, and the spotty dog dragging the case is my friend Fluke.'

'Hi...' Fluke said happily as he bent down, grabbed a pile of parchments, and handed them back to the boy. 'So what have you got here then?' he asked as he picked up another pawful of papers, wiping a bead of sweat from his brow as the heat was getting to him a bit. He caught sight of one of the rolls that had become partly unrolled. The parchment contained diagrams, sketches and lots and lots of neatly handwritten hieroglyphics notes.

'My name is Baba,' the boy said, a bit shyly, still staring at Tash, almost in awe, she thought to herself.

'There you go my friend, that's all of your belongings, you've certainly got an armful there,' Fluke said, handing over the last of the parchment rolls.

'Thank you,' Baba said and started to bow again.

'Please, no more bowing!' begged Tash, staring at Baba, 'you'll drop your papers again. Why do you keep bowing to me? I mean it's nice, don't get me wrong, but you don't even know us. Is it a local custom to greet strangers this way?'

'No, it's not a traditional custom,' Baba confirmed, 'but you do resemble Bastet, our great cat goddess, and I thought that was worth bowing down for. I mean we don't get to see a cat goddess every morning on the way to school!' He smiled and attempted to shake the paws of Fluke and Tash.

'Cat goddess?' Fluke looked Tash up and down and poked her to make sure she was real and not some mythical goddess after all. 'What about me? Do I resemble anyone famous?'

'Err, not really,' Baba said somewhat sheepishly. 'Oh, wait a minute, my dad did mention about this famous labourer once that lived in our village. Big and strong he was, and covered from head to toe in freckles, that looked a bit like your spots!'

'Ooh great!' Fluke muttered. 'She' – he jabbed his paw at Tash – 'looks like a goddess, and me,' – he pointed to himself – 'I look like a labourer. Just my luck!'

'Yes Fluke, but he was big and strong!' laughed Tash.

'So, anyway, where are you headed?' Baba asked trying to change the subject.

Tash nodded in the general direction of the village. 'We're on holiday and trying to find somewhere to stay for a few days, rest up and store our luggage, and whilst we're here we want to explore this part of Egypt and take in the local culture.'

'We want to have a ride on a camel, have a boat trip down the Nile, and see some pyramids,' Fluke carried on from where Tash left off.

'Don't forget chariot racing Fluke, you did say you wanted to go chariot racing!' continued Tash.

'Well, you'll certainly be busy then,' Baba said. 'Look, if you want, you can stay at our house. I'm sure my mum and dad won't mind, I mean to have Bastet, the cat goddess, or certainly a good lookalike, staying at our house would be an honour and keep the village talking for many days!'

'That would be cool,' Fluke said, 'it's a deal!'

'We couldn't pay any rent,' Tash interrupted, 'but I'm sure we could help out around the house to help pay our way, I mean, you've not only got a cat goddess staying, but a big burly labourer to do all the heavy lifting,' she tittered and pointed at Fluke.

'Tell you what, follow me back home. I'll introduce you to my Mum, and then I had better be off to school,' Baba said, and headed back the way he had come, with Tash hot on his heels, and Fluke following, dragging the case behind him.

Scribe school...

'So what do you study at school?' asked a curious Fluke, eager to know what the diagrams and sketches were that he had seen on the rolled up parchment papers.

'I'm in my last year at scribe school, Fluke,' Baba said, letting Fluke catch up to walk alongside. 'It's hard work, but I'm nearly a fully qualified *sesh* or *scribe* as we are better known. We get taught how to write in hieroglyphics, as not many people get the opportunity to learn. It's a skilled profession, very important, and also they teach us how to draw complicated building plans which are used during the construction of temples and pyramids.'

'Wow, pretty impressive for someone so young,' Tash said, with a hint of praise in her voice, 'we call them draughtsmen or architects back home, drawing up plans for construction projects.'

'Where is home?' asked a now curious Baba.

'Well, where do we start,' Tash said looking at Fluke, 'as you're carrying our transport Fluke, do you want to explain to young Baba how we got here?'

'Transport?' Baba eyed the case with a curious look.

'Well,' began Fluke, 'it works something like this. We're not from around here,' he did a full 360 degree turn, pointed in every direction, 'in fact we're not even from this time period at all! We've travelled here from the future, and this,' he pointed with pride to their case, 'is our very own, magic, time travelling suitcase.'

Baba didn't appear fazed by Fluke's answer, and took it all in his stride as if meeting a time-travelling dog and cat was an everyday occurrence.

'You don't seem surprised?' Tash asked Baba, glancing sideways to Fluke.

'Well, with all our ancient history, super rich and powerful Pharaohs, all our different gods that we worship and all those old paintings I've seen drawn on walls in some of the old temples, it makes me believe that anything is possible!' Baba stated. 'A lot of the paintings show some really weird stuff,' Baba continued, 'stuff that me, and my friends, don't really know what or who they are meant to be drawings of.'

'Wouldn't mind seeing some of those,' confirmed Tash, always keen and eager to expand her knowledge.

'So, if you're not from here, where are you from?' Baba asked.

'England, and quite a few years in the future let me tell you!' Fluke confirmed.

Village of Deir-el-Medina...

The three new friends had now entered the village, which was a lot larger than they first thought, having previously only viewed it from the air.

'So, does your village have a name?' asked Fluke.

'Welcome to Deir-el-Medina, or home as we also call it!' laughed Baba.

'We've heard of it, haven't we Tash?' said Fluke, 'a very famous village mentioned in all our history books,' he said breathlessly, eager to impress Baba and show him that he wasn't the only one with some sort of education.

'Famous? Why is it famous? It's just a village with buildings and people leading a normal life,' Baba said with a confused look on his face.

'It will be famous in the future, trust me, but not for many, many more years yet,' said Tash. 'Our experts will find all your temples and pyramids of great interest. They give us a huge insight into how ancient Egyptians lived, and the village of Deir-el-Medina becomes world famous! It had all the best artisan stonemasons, stone cutters, sculptors, painters and of course not forgetting the very best scribes living and working here!'

Shaking his head in bewilderment, Baba strode off, and headed towards his house, secretly hoping that some of his neighbours could see him walking with Bastet, that would make them a bit envious and give the village something to talk about!

Baba's house was constructed in a typical Egyptian way. Made of mudbrick, housed on top of stone foundations, the walls were covered in dried mud, and painted white. A wooden door opened, and out strode a lady, dressed in a traditional kalasiris. She stopped with a puzzled look on her face.

'Did you forget something Baba?' the lady called out to her son. 'Maybe you forgot your homework or your pens again?' she shook her head. 'Hanging around with that young girl Nedjem is making you go silly in the head!' though 'she's a beauty I must admit,' said Baba's mum, then stopped herself as for the first time she noticed they had visitors.

'Where's your manners boy?' she said with some irritation in her voice, 'are you not going to introduce me to your friends?' she indicated Fluke and Tash, who both stood patiently behind Baba.

'Sorry Mum,' Baba apologised, 'please meet my new friends, Fluke and Tash.'

The pair stepped forward, Tash leading the way. An audible gasp left Abana's mouth and she started to bow.

'You don't have to keep bowing to her,' Fluke said, pointing at Tash. 'She's no royal princess, and certainly isn't a goddess either, besides, she'll only get embarrassed, and all this attention is going to make her even more big headed than she normally is,' laughed Fluke.

Tash stepped up, introduced herself and shook hands with Baba's mum, Abana. Fluke followed, and also shook hands and introduced himself.

'Well, well,' she muttered turning to Baba, 'she really does look like Bastet doesn't she!' 'Come, come in,' she beckoned with her hand, 'let me make something for you to eat and drink,' and as they entered the house she turned to Baba and told him, 'Drinks and food for our guests Baba, you've got to get back to school, so hurry up you can't be late again, that will be twice this week, you'll have plenty of time this evening to hang around and play with your new friends.'

Bread and beer...

Baba was shooed out of the door and headed off to scribe school, his arms once more full of parchment papers and pens.

'No doubt he'll be late again,' muttered Abana.

Just before the door slammed shut Tash shouted: 'See you later Baba, and remember no bowing to strangers, and don't drop everything this time!'

Baba's mum busied herself in the small kitchen, and served them up a lovely breakfast, much to the delight of Fluke, who unusually for him, had not thought of food for the last couple of hours.

Abana had wanted to know all about her son's new friends and was especially interested in the magic case. She busied herself asking questions and cooking at the same time.

Breakfast consisted of sweet Egyptian flat bread covered in coriander seeds and lovely sweet dates, and beer, which, as Fluke and Tash soon learned, was a staple part of the Egyptian diet.

'Dad would love the breakfast here Tash,' said Fluke between mouthfuls of nourishing bread, washed down with some of Abana's homemade beer.

'He would,' agreed Tash, 'but beer is thought of differently here in Egypt Fluke, it's an important source of nutrition,' she said as she studied the rather cloudy looking drink, 'it's full of proteins and vitamins.' She drained the last dregs from her cup, wiping her mouth with the back of her paw and gave a contented sigh.

'So what are your plans for today?' Abana asked as the three of them cleared away the breakfast table. 'You know you two can stay for as long as you like,' she continued, 'it's not much to look at but it's comfy and it's our home.'

Fluke explained that they wanted to have a look around at some temples, see the River Nile, and hoped to take a boat trip.

'Baba can take you on an evening boat trip after school if you can wait that long?' Abana offered. 'His father's friend is a boat builder and also runs a pleasure boat service. He gives a wonderful evening boat tour, and I dare say you'll meet Baba's girlfriend Nedjem as well.'

It was agreed they would investigate the village this afternoon and wait for Baba to finish scribe school.

Fluke and Tash thanked Abana again for their hearty and nourishing breakfast, stored their magic case in their allotted bedroom and made their way out to explore the village.

'Lovely lady, that Abana,' confirmed Tash, 'and my, can she cook! I didn't realise how hungry I was until I smelt the wonderful aromas of freshly baked bread.'

'The whole family are friendly. Baba seems like a good friend to have and I'm really looking forward to meeting his Dad and tonight's boat trip,' said Fluke, striding alongside Tash heading into the village.

They passed several people making their way to work to start their daily routines; some were water carriers heading off to the nearest well to replenish their water supplies, but most appeared to be farmers working on their crops.

'You wouldn't have thought that living in a hot desert, you'd be able to grow much, especially with all this hot sand!' Fluke winced as he remembered his burning paws when they'd first arrived.

'I know we're in the desert Fluke, but the whole area is very fertile, courtesy of the River Nile. The area is prone to flooding once a year. As the floodwaters drain away, the silt left behind provides perfect soil in which to grow their crops and they've mastered the irrigation system as well. Quite a remarkable race of people these Egyptians.'

'Have you, by any chance, been reading up on this before we left home then?' said Fluke, slightly envious of the knowledge that Tash always seemed to have.

They spent a couple of hours wandering the streets, but the village houses all appeared to be the same. Once you'd seen one house you'd seen them all, and with few people around to talk to, they found themselves wandering off the beaten track and heading out of the village towards the river bank for a better view of the Nile.

'So how far away are all the temples and pyramids Tash?' Fluke asked, working his way up a slight incline, weaving his way through the thick foliage of papyrus reed beds which grew up to two metres tall. The thick wall of reeds partially blocked their views. They bent and swayed with the slight breeze giving Fluke and Tash occasional glimpses of the river, the sun reflecting off its surface giving them some magical views.

As they reached the top of a small dune they stood gazing at the river, gracefully flowing along without a care in the world; the slight breeze ruffled their coats, giving them a brief respite from the heat of the sun.

'Wow!' said Fluke, 'what a view eh Tash? I thought Sherwood Forest was spectacular, but this is magnificent.'

'Certainly is Fluke,' Tash agreed. 'It's a bit hotter than Sherwood as well!' she panted, paws resting on her hips.

'The Valley of the Kings with the pyramids is over that way somewhere,' she pointed, 'and the Valley of the Queens is a bit further in the same direction. I think most of the village artisans, builders and stone cutters are working there now Fluke, they work and sleep nearby in tents for a few days, saves a lot of time not having to travel back and forth every morning.'

'That explains why the village is a bit quiet then. Come on, let's head back and see if Baba is home yet.'

Tash agreed, and off they walked, heading back towards the village and Baba's family home.

The felucca...

Sure enough Baba was on his way home and they met in the middle of the village, Baba's delight at seeing his two new friends was evident in his beaming smile.

'Fluke, Tash, how's your day been?' said an excited Baba, 'hope my mum looked after you and fed you well?'

'She did! How was scribe school?' said Tash.

'Oh long and boring as usual, but I've finished now for two whole days!' he whooped in joy. 'Come on, follow me, I want to see if Dad's home yet, he can take us on his friend's felucca, I've been thinking about tonight and wondered if you fancied taking a boat trip on the Nile? It's lovely sailing up and down the river, especially early evening, it's so peaceful, and I want you to meet my girlfriend Nedjem, she'll come along as well, you'll like her, she's very pretty!' Tash noticed Baba blush ever so slightly.

Tash smiled, 'A boat trip would be fantastic. We did mention it earlier to your mum, who said your dad's friend had a boat.'

'You do know I can't swim?' Fluke said turning to Tash, slightly nervously, 'but I still want to go tonight, just make sure I don't fall in!'

They entered the house through the wooden door, and Fluke noticed that instead of house numbers they had a small plaque fixed to the front which was engraved with the family name.

'Hi Mum, I'm home, and I wasn't late this morning, well not by much anyway!' Baba said, throwing down his homework on the table. 'Hi Dad, how was work today?' exclaimed Baba, and before his dad could reply, Baba continued without drawing breath, 'I would like you to meet my two new friends, this is Tash, and no she's not a goddess before you ask, and this is Fluke, and again, before you ask, no he's not a relation to the famous spotty labourer you told me about!' He indicated the pair stood by the door, waiting for their introduction.

'Your mum's already told me we have guests staying.' He smiled, and walked over to introduce himself, arm outstretched to shake their paws.

'In case you didn't know,' he glanced at Baba, 'I'm Baba's dad, Salatis, and it's nice to meet Baba's friends. Any friends of my son are friends of the whole family.'

Salatis didn't need much persuading by Baba to arrange tonight's boat trip. He loved the water almost as much as his son did – it was the perfect way to relax after a hard day masterminding the construction work over at the Valley of the Kings. He was chief scribe over at the construction site. He'd prepared all the design drawings, oversaw the layout of the site and helped organise the site foreman to take care of the workers.

The whole family packed a few items of food, mainly flat breads and beer, and after collecting Nedjem from her house they all headed off to see Paneferher at his small boatyard. A few boats were moored up, tethered to poles and wooden jetties and a line of finished papyrus reed boats were standing outside, upright, like a line of soldiers on the parade ground awaiting inspection.

Baba walked alongside Nadjem, the pair holding hands. Baba introduced Fluke and Tash to Nadjem, who took an instant shine to the pair.

'Paneferher, where are you my friend?' Salatis shouted as they approached the boatyard. Paneferher strode out of his workshop and with a big grin etched on his face embraced his good friend Salatis.

'Good to see you Salatis, how's the new temple coming on?' and before Salatis could reply Paneferher turned to Abana, Baba and Nadjem and said 'Lovely to see you all, do I take it we are looking for an evening's river cruise? We offer excellent family rates and it's the best tour on the Nile!' Paneferher was a jovial man, always smiling and laughing. He then looked at Fluke and Tash, 'So we have some new additions to the family do we?'

Introductions were made and Paneferher rubbed his chin studying his boats with pride. His eyes rested on his favourite boat, a felucca, which was a long, narrow wooden boat with a flat bottom and triangular sail, ideal for picking up any wind gusting down the Nile. The boat was also equipped with oars in case the wind dropped or they had to row against the current.

Fluke followed Paneferher and stood admiring the craft. 'So you make boats then?' and glanced over his shoulder at the line of papyrus reed crafts lined up waiting to be sold. 'This one looks best,' he said returning his eyes to the felucca.

'You have a good eye for boats then? You can be my co-pilot Fluke.' Paneferher laughed again and slapped Fluke on the back, turning to Tash he said 'You can just relax and enjoy the scenery, we can't have Bastet pulling on the oars now can we, that will never do!' And then he helped escort everybody aboard, Tash immediately taking a comfy looking seat which gave her the best views.

'If we wait for ten minutes we'll have another couple of passengers, hope you don't mind?' he turned and spoke to Salatis. 'You know them anyway, Kahma the chariot builder is on a short vacation, he's booked an evening's trip with his wife, and I'm sure they won't mind sharing if you don't?'

'Kahma? My, I haven't seen him for a while. It'll be really nice to catch up again.'

'He's been really busy these last few months at the city of Pi-Ramesses. Chariot building is at its peak at the moment, what with the war against the Hittites about to start. Our great Pharaoh Ramesses II has begun his long march north, armed with 2,000 chariots and a large army of about 20,000 of our finest soldiers to confront Muwatalli II and his troops.'

Rudder problems...

They didn't have to wait too long. Kahma and his wife strolled up to the wooden jetty, met with Paneferher and Salatis, and boarded the felucca and hasty introductions were made all round. Fluke's ears pricked up at the mention of chariot building and he waited patiently to talk to Kahma. Salatis hugged his old friend and within minutes they had caught up with all the recent gossip.

'So the new temples are as grand as ever?' Kahma smiled as he passed the time with Salatis.

'Of course they are!' Salatis smiled back. 'You wouldn't expect anything else would you Kahma? I never fail to surprise and delight our great Pharaoh Ramesses II with my ingenious designs and superb craftsmanship,' he said cheekily.

'That's a fact,' Kahma laughed, 'you are, after all, chief architect to the great Ramesses, and we all know he favours you over all others. Although I understand you have a young pretender waiting to step into your rather large shoes?' he nodded in the direction of Baba, who blushed at the compliment given to him by Kahma.

'True, my friend, very true – Baba's in his last year at school, and his teacher gives him a glowing report, plus he has additional teaching from me when he comes home.' Salatis looked proudly towards his son and heir, who was sitting beside Nedjem, arm draped around her shoulder.

'That's of course if he can concentrate on his work – he has a certain distraction to contend with,' nodding towards Nedjem. 'So how's the great Pharaoh's favourite chariot builder? I've heard you've surpassed yourself this time? A new design of chariot and also a record number have been built for the upcoming war?'

'We've constructed over 2,000 war chariots this time, all of a new design. They're a two-man chariot instead of the normal three-man version. They're a lot lighter and supremely quick, which we hope will give us a big advantage over the slow and cumbersome Hittite chariots.'

Fluke, who had been helping Paneferher steer the felucca away from the jetty was listening keenly to the conversation about the new chariots and unfortunately wasn't concentrating as much as a co-pilot should. He had kept the rudder turned to full lock and the felucca did a complete 360 degree turn and started heading back towards the thick papyrus reed beds that lined the river bank. Its sails had caught the wind, fully inflated, and they had ploughed head on at some speed straight into the thickest part of the reeds, causing the boat to come to a juddering halt. Passengers and equipment went everywhere, ending up in a big heap on the floor. The only one that remained unscathed was Fluke who had seen what was coming and held onto the rudder with a firm grip.

'And you wonder why I don't let you drive the magic suitcase,' laughed Tash picking herself up, disentangling herself from everybody else on the floor of the boat, a scene which looked like a game of Twister!

'Sorry everybody, err really, really sorry, not used to steering yet,' blustered Fluke as he helped people to their feet. Everyone was in good humour and laughed off the incident, and Paneferher laughed louder than anyone else.

'Not to worry, nobody has injured themselves,' Paneferher confirmed, 'the only damage is to Fluke's pride!' Stepping over the side of the felucca into the water he beckoned Fluke, 'C'mon Fluke I need a hand to push the boat back into the water.'

Fluke jumped in without thinking of the consequences. Thankfully the water wasn't that deep and with a huge effort the pair managed to set the boat on the correct course. They both scrambled back on board, and Fluke regained control of the rudder, this time paying attention, and guided the felucca a safe distance away from the river bank.

It was a beautiful evening: the sun was low in the sky and the heat of the day was not as intense as earlier. Everybody seemed to be talking about the forthcoming war with the Hittite army.

Fluke asked if Paneferher could take over the rudder so he could join Kahma and Salatis talking about chariots. 'Were Kahma's new two-man chariots going to be a match for the Hittite's three-man chariots? Was the new lightweight design going to help or hinder in the heat of battle?'

'Some sensible questions from somebody with little or no knowledge of chariots Fluke, I am impressed,' Kahma said truthfully, 'you could have been a great help at the design stage!'

Tash and Baba joined in. 'Fluke and Tash would love to have a go in one, Kahma,' said Baba, 'do you think you might be able to arrange it?'

'I could young man, yes I could, but it's a long way back to my main workshop in the city of Pi-Ramesses, several days' travel by camel in fact.'

'They can use their magic suitcase to get you there very quickly, can't you Tash?' Baba looked at Tash for confirmation.

'Magic what case?' said a confused looking Kahma, 'what's one of those then?'

'Well...' started Tash, 'it's kind of like our own chariot. It's nothing compared to your new design I'm sure, but it's our own method of transport and it's how we got here in the first place.'

'This I have to see,' Kahma said rubbing his chin, 'we'll have a discussion in the morning and see what can be arranged then.'

The night was drawing in and the evening was getting cooler. Night time in the desert can get quite cold so it was agreed it was time to head back home. The wind had dropped slightly but as they turned the felucca back around, they used the currents of the Nile to glide slowly back the way they had come.

Paneferher suggested humorously, that as a penalty for ramming his boat headlong into the reeds, Fluke was to be handed an oar and made to put some back-breaking work into getting them home quicker. Paneferher got another oar and joined in with Fluke, who took it all in good spirit and was quite enjoying himself, sat alongside Paneferher they sang some Egyptian war songs, the whole party joined in the singing and Tash took her turn at the rudder and managed to guide them home safely without any mishaps.

They landed back at the boatyard, and as they parted it was agreed that Kahma would pop round in the morning to see this new chariot of Fluke and Tash's, as curiosity was getting to him.

Not what we expected...

The bright morning sun shone at such an early time of the day, early for Fluke anyway, who wanted a lie in. Sunlight streamed through the open window which made it impossible for extra sleep. He then remembered the conversation from last night. They were having guests round to see the magic suitcase and if all went well, they could soon be visiting the city of Pi-Ramesses to visit the chariot factory. That was if they could persuade Kahma to hop on the case and travel with them! Fluke jumped out of his bed, threw on his shendyt and wandered into the kitchen, only to find the whole family and Tash already seated round the breakfast table. Kahma was already there, eagerly waiting for Fluke to make an appearance.

'Morning Fluke,' the whole table said in unison. Kahma rose and shook paws with a bleary eyed Fluke.

'Sleep well?' he asked. 'I know I always do when I return home from the city. Too much noise there and back here it's so peaceful and quiet, all the fresh air and smells from the River Nile as well, I really can't wait for the war to finish and then

I can move back home for good!' Kahma said longingly.

'Anyway, that's for the future! Now show me this chariot of yours, I've been thinking about this all morning, something that travels as fast as Baba has indicated has me curious!'

Tash disappeared into the spare room and returned a few seconds later, dragging their case behind her. The room hushed as both Kahma and Salatis stood either side of the case, looking bewildered. A lot of head scratching and chin rubbing ensued.

'Now, don't take this the wrong way, but it's not quite what I was expecting!' Kahma said honestly. 'So this chariot is your transport...' he said, brow furrowed, 'and according to Baba it goes really fast?'

'How does it work, I mean how do you fix it to the horses? Does it even need horses to pull it along?' Salatis threw a couple of questions into the mix, and was equally as confused as Kahma.

Baba laughed out loud, 'Well, well, the two smartest people I know flummoxed by a dog and cat's chariot!'

Tash stepped in and started to explain as best she could. 'In all honesty we don't know how it works!' Opening the case she withdrew the old booklet and showed both Kahma and Salatis the contents, page after page of co-ordinates. 'You use one set of the small dials on top of the case to set your destination and the other set is used to calculate the time you want to arrive.'

A few more minutes were spent studying the interior, both discussing the locks, dials and the general exterior of the case before a bewildered Kahma gave in. 'It beats me I'm afraid,' he grinned at Fluke and Tash, 'but if it works as well as Baba has said, we should be able to pop back to Pi-Ramesses in no time at all.'

It was universally agreed they would see out the rest of the weekend, Kahma wanting to spend a bit more time with his wife before they headed back to his workshop in Pi-Ramesses. This worked out well for everyone, as Fluke pointed out, 'So that means we get to spend some more time here with you guys,' nodding his head towards Baba and his family. 'Maybe we can come with you to the Valley of the Kings?' He hoped he didn't sound too pushy, but both Fluke and Tash were eager to visit the pyramids and see where Salatis worked.

'Of course you can,' Salatis confirmed. 'We are always on the lookout for strong labourers,' he laughed, carrying on the *big strong labourer* theme that Baba had started yesterday.

Valley of the Kings...

Rahma bustled off back home, and agreed he would be back in a couple of days to pick up Fluke and Tash. Abana meanwhile made a packed lunch and Salatis, Baba, Fluke and Tash headed off to the Valley of the Kings. Fluke took charge of the packed lunch, putting all their food and beer in a kind of leather rucksack and strapping it to his back.

Technically it was Salatis's long weekend, but he agreed to show them around the construction site and wanted to introduce them to his site foreman, Ishpi, the man that Salatis trusted to run the site in his absence. These projects took years to finish, and the number of workers involved was huge.

The Valley of Kings was hugely impressive: spread out before them was a fine array of temples, pyramids and the whole site was a hive of activity. Work started early in the morning before the intense heat of the sun made it too hot to go on.

They all headed towards the main camp site; tents of all shapes and sizes were positioned and spaced evenly apart. Tash could see the tents were positioned in neat orderly lines and not just randomly pitched. Everything about the whole site indicated precision and order and it was obvious it ran like clockwork.

'Ishpi, my good friend, let me introduce you to some new friends of Baba's who are staying with us for a few days.' Salatis had found his foreman studying some new building plans that had been drawn up by Salatis just before he went on leave. The plans were on traditional parchment paper and had been laid out on a table inside the main tent that doubled up as their site hut. Ishpi was a man mountain who must be well over six feet tall and reminded Fluke of Little John.

Ishpi put down his paperwork, walked around the table and beamed a smile that filled his whole face. 'So you can't keep away then Salatis? Do you not trust your loyal foreman to do a good job whilst you're on leave?' he joked. 'You'll find everything in order that I promise you!' Still smiling he approached Baba and shook him warmly by the hand. 'So when can we expect the great Baba to join us then? We've all heard great things about your schooling, your dad has been telling us how good a scribe you've become, the new future chief architect to Ramesses II, I dare say!'

Baba blushed again, the grown-ups made a habit of embarrassing him in public. 'A little while yet I'm afraid,' Baba confirmed. 'Ishpi, please meet my new friends Fluke and Tash, they've come to lend a hand for a couple of days.' He moved aside and let Ishpi run his eye up and down the newcomers.

'You certainly look like you could help out our stonemasons with a bit of labouring,' he said as he shook Fluke by his paw, 'quite a physical job mind you, but you look like you can handle the workload.' With a grin etched on his face he turned to Tash and made a mock bow, 'we are graced by the presence of our royal cat goddess, Bastet!' he joked. 'The only thing is, I think you're a bit smaller than we all pictured, but a very good likeness nevertheless.'

Tash laughed. 'Well thank you Ishpi, if I wasn't a bit paranoid about my height I certainly am now!'

Fluke laughed out loud, 'Come on tiny, move out the way and let the adults have a look at the building plans, we've got some work to be getting on with!' and he moved alongside Ishpi to study the plans. After a couple of minutes of silence and a lot of head scratching, it dawned on Fluke and everybody else watching that he didn't have a clue what he was looking at.

'Fluke, it might actually help if you turned the plans up the right way round, we always find it easier that way!' said Ishpi and the whole room burst out laughing.

'I thought it all looked a bit strange, mind you, even the right way round all I can see are lots of lines and handwritten notes. I think I'll leave the drawings to the experts and concentrate on manual labour instead!' He moved out of the way, letting Salatis move alongside Ishpi to discuss the next phase of work they had started this morning.

After a couple of minutes discussing part of the drawing, Ishpi and Salatis took Fluke and Tash on a quick tour of the site, pointing out some older pyramids built for past Pharaohs. They certainly were jaw dropping, and the history lesson was very interesting.

Salatis pointed to one pyramid in particular, 'That's Seti I's pyramid. He was our current Pharaoh's father, who sadly passed away four years ago, but he was a great leader. Ramesses II has taken a lot of his leadership qualities and learnt a lot from his father. Are you listening Baba? Yes, believe it or not, actually listening to your father can make you a better person!'

'Yeah, ok Dad I know, I do listen to you, well sometimes anyway!'

Salatis smiled and continued, 'The one a bit further away is the pyramid of Ramesses I, Seti I's father, and several more pyramids that are really old, going way back.'

It was pointed out that in the next valley was the Valley of the Queens, where the royal wives of the Pharaohs were buried, such as Tanedjemet and Sitre, royal wives of Seti I and Ramesses I respectively.

'Well, come along you two, can't waste any more time, we have work to do, you'll be giving me a bad reputation as an easy going foreman and I can't have that, I've got my reputation to think of!' laughed Ishpi.

'No certainly not, no slacking on Ishpi's watch that I can certainly vouch for, he doesn't even let me rest for too long and I'm his boss!' Salatis confirmed.

Brick laying on
a grand scale...

Salatis and Baba stayed behind to concentrate on the new construction drawings, whilst Ishpi took Fluke and Tash over to the main construction site. There were a few pyramids and other temples under construction, but the main one they had slowed down in front of towered over all the others.

'Wow,' muttered Fluke nudging Tash as they both stared up at the nearly completed pyramid, 'will you look at the size of it.' He stopped in his tracks and stood gazing up.

Tash, equally in awe, heartily agreed, 'It must have taken ages to construct something this grand.' Turning to Ishpi, she asked, 'How do you get the stones up to the top? I can't see a crane or lifting gear anywhere!'

'With a lot of brute force, sore hands and plenty of aching backs,' Ishpi smiled at Tash. 'If you look closely,' pointing at another pyramid that was only half completed, 'you can see we've made sloping ramps or paths that coil their way around the outside of the pyramid, gradually getting steeper as it winds its way to the top. We literally have to drag the stones up these ramps on sledges and then manhandle the stones into position.'

'Crickey, you must use some seriously strong slave labour to haul the stones up those ramps,' said Fluke studying a small group of men dragging the sledge up a steep incline.

'No slave labour here Fluke, we only use the finest stonemasons and stone cutters on all of our construction sites.' Ishpi pointed all around with pride at his large workforce. 'Our illustrious Pharaoh quite simply demands we use top quality materials and employ the best tradesmen. He wants his temples to be the very best there is and be remembered for years to come.'

'Well that counts us out of any hard work then,' Tash breathed a sigh of relief, 'I mean we're hardly stonemasons and we're definitely not expert tradesmen!'

'Oh, don't you worry about that, I'm sure we can make an exception for you two,' laughed Ishpi. 'Come on, let me take you over and introduce you to my men working on that large sledge at the bottom of the ramp, you can help them fasten the stone securely and then help haul it to the top!' He strode off, his two new temporary employees following close on his heels.

Ishpi introduced his new apprentices to his workers, who grateful for a short break, stopped strapping the big stone to the sledge and gave Fluke and Tash a warm welcome. Ishpi explained the techniques involved in securing the stone safely, through weight distribution and making sure the ropes were tied tightly to prevent the stone falling off halfway up the ramp.

'You wouldn't want that stone falling off!' commented Fluke, looking down at his sandals, shuddering at the thought of the huge stone landing on his paws.

'If it's going to happen to anybody Fluke, it's bound to be you!' Tash confirmed what Fluke was already thinking. 'You've already got burnt paws from the scorching hot sand!'

Ishpi reassured Fluke that the stone wouldn't fall off and let his men take over. Standing back with his arms folded, he was content in the knowledge that the stone slab would soon be in its correct position midway up the side of the pyramid. Fluke was shown how to secure the rope on one side of the sledge, whilst Tash was taught how to fasten a secure knot to the other side. The stone slab wasn't going anywhere except on the back of the sledge.

As instructed by Ishpi, Fluke and Tash strode to the front of the sledge and grabbed hold of the sturdy length of rope which was securely fixed

one end and knotted at intervals down its length, the knots providing a good place to grip the rope and prevent it from slipping out of their paws.

Ten men were generally used to help manoeuvre the sledge up the incline of the ramp, which Tash initially thought wouldn't be enough manpower to budge the heavy stone, let alone drag it uphill, but as it turned out she was pleasantly surprised. Water was used to lubricate the sand on the ramp which helped to reduce any friction, and as they all took the strain, muscles tensed in anticipation, Ishpi gave the command and they all started pulling at once, and the mighty stone began its journey up the sloping ramp.

'C'mon Tash, heave-ho, and pull like you've never pulled before!' puffed Fluke, sweat pouring down his face.

'You know,' wheezed Tash, 'I always pictured slaves pulling the sledge, with some burly oaf walking alongside holding a big whip, lashing the slaves to within an inch of their lives, being encouraged to pull harder and faster, but it's not like that at all, it's actually very civilised and well organised.'

Fluke was in deep conversation with his fellow workers and lost track of time on how long they had been pulling the sledge, but before long the command was given to stop, and thankfully they released the rope and stood slightly bent over, paws on hips, gasping for breath.

'I'm so unfit,' panted Tash, looking over at Fluke hoping she wasn't the only one out of breath. She was relieved to see that Fluke was just as bad, but the rest of the work party seemed remarkably fresh, which was just as well as they had to repeat this task several times a day.

The straps were untied and the huge stone sat there on the sledge waiting to be offloaded. Fluke and Tash were handed long, sturdy looking wooden poles to help lever the stone off of the sledge and into position for the stonemasons to start their work. On the count of three they all used their poles and the stone slid into position, and with a bit of manhandling the stone was finally in place.

The Nummer stonemasons...

Tash nudged Fluke. 'Well look who is here Fluke, it's some of the Nummers working as stonemasons!'

Fluke looked over and sure enough a large work party of small, but stocky looking Nummers were hard at work, swarming all over the stone, lining it up with all the previously laid stones. Working hard with their tools, chipping bits off with their heavy looking chisels, they used string lines to make sure the stone was perfectly level and everything lined up.

'Hi there,' Fluke walked over and introduced themselves, 'I'm Fluke and she's Tash.' The Nummers briefly stopped work, leant on their tools and introduced themselves.

'I'm Maya, the head stone cutter, and this is Hapu, who likes to think he's the head sculptor!' Maya said, a huge grin spread over his face as he engaged the pair in a conversation. Tash explained about the Nummers back home and passed on their good wishes and Fluke wanted to know a bit about their work.

'We can tell you Fluke...' said Hapu, 'but it's just as easy to show you,' he laughed, and asked Ishpi to hand Fluke a heavy looking mallet and chisel. The mallet was so heavy that Fluke wasn't prepared for the weight of it, and let it slip from his sweaty paw. The mallet fell and headed for his sandals, and realisation dawned on Fluke that it was going to hurt. He let out a yelp of pain as it caught his paw full on and bounced off. Hopping up and down clutching his sore paw, Fluke removed the sandal and rubbed his paw vigorously, more in embarrassment than anything else.

'Ouch, I felt that,' winced Tash who bent down to retrieve the mallet and handed the offending tool to Fluke, who this time wasn't going to let it happen again and held firmly onto the handle.

'All part of the job I suppose!' he grinned, slipping his paw back inside the sandal and turning back to Hapu for some on the spot training in stonemasonry.

Tash was handed a mallet and chisel as well and they set to work in shaping the stone under the watchful gaze of Ishpi, Maya and Hapu. They quickly got into a steady rhythm and before long they stood back to admire their handiwork.

'Not bad, not bad at all!' praised Ishpi, 'we'll make half decent stonemasons out of you I'm sure.' The praise from Ishpi caused Fluke and

Tash to blush, and the incident of Fluke's sore paw was soon forgotten.

As the day wore on several more stones were brought up from the foot of the pyramid, the exercise was repeated for each stone, and by the end of the day they had laid a whole new line of stone. They all downed tools for the day and stood back to admire their work.

'How are you feeling after your first day?' Ishpi asked. 'It's hard work but hopefully you're not aching too much!'

'Not aching at the moment,' confirmed Tash, 'but I think tomorrow morning we might be!'

They called it a day. Fluke and Tash said their thanks to Maya, Hapu and the rest of the Nummers for their day's training in stonemasonry, and the Nummers said their goodbyes and asked Tash to pass on their good wishes to the Nummers back home. All the workers packed away their tools, strode off down the ramp pulling the sledge with them into the setting sun and headed for their camp site, ready for their evening's rest, leaving Fluke, Tash and Ishpi behind.

'Stunning views from up here,' said Fluke spinning a full turn, noticing the colour of the landscape had changed from earlier on in the day. As the sun was setting behind one of the distant pyramids and slowly disappearing below the horizon, the harsh glare from the mid-day sun had been replaced with softer shades of red and orange. A few stray white clouds in the sky painted wonderful shapes on what could have easily been an artist's canvas.

'I never knew hard work could be so enjoyable!' said Tash. Turning to Ishpi she continued, 'You've got some wonderful workers Ishpi, they're very good at what they do.'

'Very patient teachers as well!' Fluke confirmed. 'They'd have to be to want to spend time teaching us two!' he grinned.

'Nonsense, you've both done remarkably well today, but enough for now, time to make our way back to camp and see what Salatis and Baba have been doing whilst we've been working,' and all three walked back down the ramp and headed off towards camp.

'I'm hungry Tash!' said Fluke, who for the first time today had actually had time to think about his stomach and lack of food.

For once Tash was in complete agreement. 'Must admit I could do with a snack or two, we've got to keep up our energy levels for tomorrow!' The pair picked up the pace causing Ishpi to lengthen his stride and quicken his pace just to keep up.

Painters and decorators...

Baba ran over to greet the returning workers and wanted to know all the details of what they had been doing. Their day was explained in great detail and with much enthusiasm and Baba was asked what he and Salatis had been doing.

'Of all the things I could be doing, can you believe my dad has me working on his new drawings!' laughed Baba. 'Still I shouldn't complain, at least I didn't have a heavy mallet drop on my feet!' and with that everybody in the tent laughed, Ishpi louder than anybody else.

The laughing subsided and Ishpi put his strong arms around Fluke and Tash. 'These two have worked so hard today, I'm really proud of them and if they wanted to stay longer I wouldn't hesitate in offering them full training and long term employment!'

'So what can we do tomorrow that doesn't involve anything that could cause harm to my already sore paws?' Fluke joked.

Salatis smiled and looked up from his drawings, 'How about some painting? You could help some of our master craftsmen inside one of the pyramids.'

'I've always fancied myself as an artist,' grinned Fluke.

So it was agreed, tomorrow they would be painting and decorating. 'Not only can we release our artistic nature but it will also be a lot cooler inside!' said Tash.

'Well that's tomorrow sorted,' said Ishpi, 'but before we all pass out with hunger I would suggest we go and grab some well-earned dinner before the hungry hordes eat it all!' So they all trooped off and headed towards the catering tent, a huge structure that was home to the cooks and all the staff who kept up the constant supply of food for the workers.

Fluke's nose began to twitch at the wonderful smells and aromas that escaped from the tent, his stomach rumbled at the thought of the feast to come. As they entered the tent they saw the Nummers sitting in a group, plates full of nourishing and hearty food. They exchanged greetings once again, and then Fluke and Tash were steered by Salatis towards the food; the queue was long but moved quickly.

They were treated to a lavish feast of meat and freshly caught fish from the River Nile, accompanied by a host of vegetables such as garlic, green spring onions, green peas, beans and lentils, which together made up a healthy stew. The standard hearty bread was used to mop up any of the juices, and a jug of the rather tasty local beer, packed full of proteins and a staple part of the Egyptian diet, washed everything down quite nicely!

Fluke rubbed his now full belly and let out a quiet burp, 'Sorry, didn't mean to be rude that just slipped out! That dinner was delicious.' Tash heartily agreed.

There was a babble of noise all around the tent, people coming in, and people leaving, most making their way to their beds. All the food was consumed, every plate and bowl was clean, not a morsel of food left to waste, a real compliment to the cooks.

Tash and Fluke stood, and the rest of their party followed as they bid farewells to the people sitting next to them, freeing up space for any newcomers wanting to eat, and headed back to their accommodation for the evening.

The tent they had been allocated was basic but had the most important item they could wish for – large comfy bedding, and it didn't take too long to get settled.

'Night Fluke,' yawned Tash, snuggling up under her soft Egyptian cotton sheets, 'another big day tomorrow to look forward to.' But Fluke had already dozed off, and was soon followed by Tash.

The artists...

Tash woke early, sprang out of bed and performed her morning stretching exercises, desperate to ease the aches and pains that her body felt after their hard day's work with the Nummers and the rest of the gang yesterday.

'Wakey-wakey!' said Tash a bit too chirpily for Fluke. He wasn't a morning dog, and didn't understand people who seemed to wake up full of beans. He lay under his bedding watching Tash carry out her morning work-out routine.

'Crikey, it's like watching one of the exercise videos that Mum watches at home trying to keep fit!' laughed Fluke as he stumbled out of bed and made his way out of the tent, closely followed by a rejuvenated Tash, both now ready for a day of painting and decorating. They bumped into Salatis who was already busy, bent over his drawings deep in concentration.

Salatis looked up from his work, 'Ah, good morning, and how are you two feeling today?' he beamed. 'Not too sore I hope?'

'No, we're both fine, a good night's sleep certainly helps!' said Tash. 'No Baba this morning then?' queried Tash.

'I've got him running some errands for me, I have to make use of him somehow!' said Salatis. 'He'll be back later for dinner.'

'So what's the plan today?' asked Fluke, eager to get started.

'Ishpi will be here shortly, he's found one of his best painters for you to work with today, he's the master craftsman working in the Grand Ramesses pyramid – you should learn a lot today, he's very good.'

Sure enough, seconds later Ishpi strode into the tent, deep in conversation with his chief painter. 'Oh so you decided to get up at long last then...' laughed Ishpi, noticing Fluke and Tash – 'we've already done half a day's work whilst you two have been snoring merrily away!'

'Ignore him!' Salatis smiled and turned to his foreman, 'I think they both deserved a lie in this morning after a day being bossed around by you!'

Ishpi laughed, 'Yes you're probably right there!' and turned to his colleague that had followed him into the tent. 'Fluke, Tash, meet Nebitka, he'll be training you today. He's without doubt the best artist and painter that I've ever come across, and there isn't anything he doesn't know about paint.'

'No pressure then!' smiled Nebitka, and shook their paws. 'So what experience do you two have?'

'Err, none!' replied Tash, 'but we're keen and eager to learn.'

'Well, Ishpi informs me you're both quick learners so we should have you trained in the basics pretty soon.' He steered Fluke and Tash out of the tent and headed towards the large Pyramid of Ramesses.

Tash looked over her shoulder at Salatis and Ishpi, 'See you two later, and if we're any good we'll paint your portrait!' she said then quickly followed the departing Fluke out of the tent.

The heat from the mid-morning desert was hot and humid and a constant supply of fluids was essential to avoid dehydration. Fluke and Tash, who both missed breakfast due to oversleeping, made amends and took with them a packed lunch thoughtfully prepared by Baba before he went to run errands for Salatis.

They approached the Ramesses pyramid and no matter how many times you saw it, the sheer size and scale of the structure took your breath away. It was nearly finished, swarms of workers, including several hundred Nummers, were busy working away.

Outer casing stones of highly polished white limestone had been used to give the effect of a smooth finish. The casing stones had been cut to a high degree of accuracy and were laid precisely over the huge granite and limestone blocks used to create the main structure.

They entered the pyramid through an access tunnel and Fluke could feel the air change around him: it was a lot cooler in here than the outside temperature, and it got colder the deeper underground they went; the floor continued to slope away from them as they continued to follow Nebitka.

The tunnel seemed to change direction a few times, zigzagging left then right, which reminded Tash a little bit of the inner corridors back in Nottingham Castle. They arrived into the main burial chamber that would eventually house the great Ramesses when his time came.

'Phew,' whistled Fluke 'it's big isn't it?' They stopped and gazed around the room, which if it had been empty could have been quite eerie. Thankfully, a large number of craftsmen were still at work down here. Whilst most of the exterior work was nearly finished, the remaining workers inside the pyramid were still busy painting, producing some wonderful artwork that adorned the walls all around them.

Paintings of everyday life were depicted in such great detail. A huge array of colours was used and each image so life like, it seemed to Tash that they were nearly as good as a photograph. Paintings of Ramesses and his family members, his many wives, sons and daughters, were everywhere. There were paintings of the great River Nile, the life blood of Egypt, teeming with grand royal boats, and the smaller feluccas that tradesmen and pleasure boat owners used were passing in both directions.

Some scenes detailed battles that Ramesses and his father Seti had fought and Fluke noticed with interest that a couple of the battle scenes showed the old three-man chariots previously used. He wondered if after the next battle they would add some of the new two-man chariots that their friend and chariot builder Kahma had designed.

They could have spent hours gazing at the walls, but Nebitka caught their attention by making a polite coughing noise.

'When you're ready...?' he indicated with his hand a new, unpainted wall just being prepared for some artwork. 'This is the new wall that I'll be working on for the next few days, so if you want you can give me a hand...'

'Just let us know what you want from us, and we'll help anyway we can,' said Tash, as eager to start as much as Fluke was. 'You better get Fluke an apron of some sort, because he's bound to spill paint down his top!' laughed Tash.

'Oh you won't be painting straight away,' confirmed Nebitka, 'you've got to learn some basics first and then I'll introduce you to a paint brush!' He gave some instructions to some fellow workers and asked them to bring over what looked like a large stone pestle and mortar, similar, but much larger Tash thought, to the one at home that Mum used to grind up herbs and spices for dinner.

'What's cooking then?' Fluke joked, thinking the same as Tash, 'I'm assuming we're not preparing some spices for dinner then?'

'No, not dinner yet Fluke, that's later!' said Nebitka with a smile. 'We use the stone mortar to grind up minerals that make the paint' he indicated around him.

'I must admit, it never actually crossed my mind to wonder where you get the paint from,' Tash said scratching her head, 'I mean at home we pop down the shop and it's ready made in tins, but you of course don't have any garden centres or DIY stores, I guess we just take it for granted, whereas you actually have to make your own paint from scratch. Pretty impressive!'

The blue Dalmatian...

Nebitka took the stone mortar and began filling it with some minerals that his colleague had brought in. First in the large mortar went some calcium carbonate, which, Nebitka explained, was extracted from limestone and chalk. Next into the mortar went some calcium sulphate.

'The trick here...' Nebitka said grinding away with the large stone pestle... 'is to get the quantity of each mineral right. If you add more of one mineral the colour changes ever so slightly, and what we're trying to make here...' he continued, deep in concentration... 'is a white paint.'

'What exactly will we be painting today?' asked Fluke.

'We're going to show a scene from the River Nile, Fluke. We try to paint a story, and we'll detail how important the Nile is to us, it's our lifeblood. It helps crops grow and is a major way of transportation and travel as well. We'll show how our local tradesmen use the river to deliver food and supplies, we'll paint feluccas sailing up and down carrying their crops to the markets. The traders on the feluccas wear the wrap around skirts or shendyt, same clothing as you're wearing Fluke, and we're going to paint their clothing white.'

Tash was watching Nebitka intently, desperate to get stuck in and have a go. 'Fascinating watching you work; how many different colours can you make?'

'Quite a few Tash, we use shades of red and brown to paint male bodies, shades of yellow for the women, and gold to represent our gods. Blue is used to represent the heavens and the Nile, and like I said you can change the shades ever so slightly by adding in more or less of the minerals.'

Nebitka finished off mixing the white paint by finally adding water and a wood gum, which helped as an adhesive, to make sure the paint stuck to the walls once it was brushed on.

'Here you go Tash, your turn now...' Nebitka handed over the now cleaned out mortar, fresh and ready for a new batch of paint. 'I want you to make up some reddish brown paint for the male bodies of the traders steering their feluccas up and down the river.'

Tash took the stone mortar and put in some red ochre, which she learnt from Nebitka was an earth pigment and contained iron oxide, taken from the mineral hematite. Different colours of ochre could also be made: you could get yellow, purple and browns. She ground away, and when instructed by Nebitka added just the right quantity of water and wood gum. She handed back the mortar, the paint removed and stored ready for use, and the mortar was once again thoroughly cleaned.

Next it was Fluke's turn, he was making blue for the River Nile. He looked into the clean mortar bowl and added in azurite, a deep blue, copper based mineral, and ground away using his heavy stone pestle which easily mixed up the minerals. Unfortunately, in his eagerness to impress his new boss he got a bit carried away. Staring intently at the bottom of the mortar, his face was a bit close to the stone bowel. He was grinding too vigorously, and flecks of blue powder flew out of the mortar and covered his face. Unaware of what had happened he looked up proudly to hand the mortar back to Nebitka.

Tash couldn't help herself, and laughed out loud. 'I think we've just discovered a new breed of Dalmatian.'

'What are you on about?' said a confused Fluke who looked around the room trying to see what Tash meant, fully expecting to see another dog enter the chamber.

Everyone Fluke looked at joined in with Tash and started laughing.

'What's so funny, come on you guys let me into the joke...'

'I've never a seen a Dalmatian with *blue* spots before,' said Tash, now rolling around the chamber floor in fits of giggles.

Nebitka was laughing too, and explained, 'It's your face, Fluke... How can I put it politely? You've managed to cover yourself in blue powder. You've managed to get more paint on your face than what you've got left in the mortar.'

One of Nebitka's workers walked over and kindly handed Fluke a cloth to clean himself up and wipe away the blue powder.

'Yeah, well I like to be different and try the paint before we cover the walls in it,' laughed Fluke, now joining in the fun.

'It suited you Fluke, although I'm not sure if it will ever catch on,' said Tash eventually regaining her composure.

'Right, now let's see if it looks better on the walls than it did on your face,' said Nebitka with a grin.

Painting by numbers...

More paint was mixed and stored, ready to be used for the painting that was about to take shape on the blank stone wall.

Nebitka asked Tash to pass him the rolled up papyrus that was on the floor by her side. Unrolling the sheet, Nebitka showed Tash and Fluke the draft sketches that would be copied onto the wall. The sketch was a scene taken from the Nile. Feluccas were sailing up and down delivering goods, vegetation and crops were growing on the banks of the Nile, and at the centre was a royal barge with its cargo of passengers – the great Pharaoh Ramesses II and his family.

Nebitka explained, 'We sketch our drawing on the papyrus and then map out horizontal and vertical grid lines over the top... 'We number each square, then apply the grid system to the wall on a larger, scaled up version of the grid lines on the paper. Finally, we copy the images from the paper onto the wall.'

'Pretty smart thinking...' said Tash, clearly impressed, 'an early case of painting by numbers.'

'Come on, I'll need a hand to mark up the grid on the wall.' Nebitka walked over to the wall and was handed a rolled up bunch of string by one of his colleagues.

'What's the string for?' asked Fluke.

Unrolling a length of the string, Nebitka handed one end to Fluke, measured the wall, cut the string to the required length, and handed the other end to Tash.

'Fluke, if you could take your end of string to the far end, and Tash if you take yours to the opposite end please,' Nebitka instructed the pair. 'The string is covered in red paint. If you pull as tight as you can to stretch the string and hold it up against the wall it will leave a faint red horizontal line.'

Sure enough, a perfect faint red horizontal line was left behind. The process was repeated several times, one line above the other, each horizontal line was evenly spaced apart, until the number of lines on the wall matched the number of lines on the papyrus.

Next it was the turn of the vertical lines. Fluke, being taller than Tash, stretched, and reached up as far as he could to hold his end of string at the top of the wall. Tash bent down and held her end of string at the base of the wall. Again, the process was repeated from left to right across the wall, until the vertical lines matched the papyrus roll.

Fluke stood back and studied the perfectly formed grid. He counted a total of 50 squares – five rows, with each row containing ten squares. Glancing over at the papyrus to double check, he was relieved to also count 50 squares on there as well.

Nebitka double checked their handiwork and confirmed they were now ready to paint. He handed two brushes to his budding new artists, and asked Fluke to start in the top left hand square, whilst Tash being shorter was asked to start in the bottom right hand corner.

'What are the brushes made from?' queried Tash studying her paint brush.

'Reeds...' Nebitka said as he looked at his own paintbrush, 'all bunched up and bound together. The ends are mashed up a little bit to soften them, making them pliable and easier to use.'

They were then each handed a wooden palette containing six different colours. Tash looked at the image in the bottom right hand square from the original draft sketch, dipped her brush into some paint and started dabbing the paint onto the wall. Fluke was deep in concentration, his tongue poking out the side of his mouth as he too began his masterpiece: his section of the wall would be the blue sky.

Under the watchful gaze and expert tuition of Nebitka, the painting slowly took shape. The blue sky had been painted in by Fluke, and Tash had completed most of the river bank.

Tash, whilst painting her own section, had closely been watching Nebitka, whose painting skills were excellent, to see if she could pick up any more tips. She stood back to admire her own handiwork, and looked over to Fluke's section of the wall. He had finished the blue sky and was now busily attempting to paint some human figures sailing in one of the feluccas. Now Tash knew that painting people's faces was extremely difficult, and anybody that attempted the difficult task should be applauded, but looking at Fluke's efforts she couldn't help but chuckle to herself. His first attempt resembled a stick man – yes, we've all drawn them at some point in our lives – and his second attempt at someone's face was literally a round circle, two dots for the eyes and a triangle for the nose.

'Hmm,' said Tash rubbing her chin as if in deep, critical, thought, 'you've got feeling in your work Fluke, it's obvious to see, dog and brush in perfect harmony, the way you've managed to bring your work to life, it's quite an achievement,' she giggled.

Fluke missed the sarcasm and carried on painting.

'You think so?' he said proudly, continuing his best efforts.

'Well, I certainly think you could give Leonardo da Vinci and Michelangelo a run for their money,' Tash said and then fell about laughing as she couldn't keep a straight face any longer.

'Oh, so you were joking then?' Fluke stood back and gave his *masterpiece* work a critical once over and then burst out laughing himself.

'Yeah I guess you're right Tash, better leave the arty stuff to the experts!' and watched as one of Nebitka's workers painted over Fluke's *Stick men* people and finished off the boat scene with a more recognisable human face.

Camel racing...

They called it a day, downed brushes, cleaned themselves, brushes and paint palette and thanked Nebitka for the tuition.

'We really appreciate your help today,' Nebitka said.

'I tell you, it's a lot harder than it looks,' said Fluke as they discussed their day's painting whilst walking back to camp.

They met up with Baba and exchanged stories of their eventful day.

'Good news you two...' Baba said excitedly, 'I've been home running errands for Dad, and ran into Kahma who asked me to pass on a message to say he's ready for his trip back to his workshop in Pi-Ramesses, that's if you still want to go?'

'Yeah!' said Fluke keenly, 'can't wait – oh just think Tash we'll have a go at making some chariots tomorrow!'

'We're turning into some real experts...' Tash said, 'stonemasons, painters and soon to be carpenters!'

Their last evening back at camp was going to be eventful. Salatis had organised some camel racing as Baba had told his dad that Fluke and Tash wanted to ride a camel.

Dinner was hastily consumed in the large catering tent, then Salatis took them over to meet the camels and greet some of the other riders taking part in the racing.

'So which camels are we riding...?' asked Fluke excitedly, rubbing his paws together in anticipation of the race that was to follow. 'Those two over there look a bit short for camels...' pointing to a couple of the dromedaries close by, 'the ones next to them are a lot taller,' he noted.

'They're down on their knees Fluke...' laughed Tash, 'just wait till they stand up, trust me they will be tall enough for you.'

'C'mon you two, time to meet your camels, and listen carefully to their handlers. They'll give you some instructions on riding techniques and how to hang on, as the camel isn't the easiest animal to ride!' Salatis steered them over to the waiting Bedouin tribesmen.

Instructions were given. Tash was listening carefully and taking in everything she was being told, as she had no intentions of falling off. Her competitive nature was also coming out, she may not win the race, but she was desperate to beat Fluke!

'Have you been listening Fluke?' asked Tash, noting that Fluke was only half listening. He was gazing all around the camp, soaking up the atmosphere.

'Fluke, you'll be riding the bull and Tash you've got the cow,' confirmed Salatis.

'Bull?' said Fluke warily, suddenly paying attention, shuddering despite the heat as he remembered his recent experience with the bull at Nottingham castle.

Tash laughed, 'The male camel is called a bull, the females are called cows and the infants are calves – don't fret Fluke, it's not the type of bull you've had recent problems with!'

A circular track had been laid out in the sand. Flaming torches were spaced to form a huge circle. The racing track, Tash estimated, must be at least 400m round from start to finish – it looked similar in size to an Olympic running track.

Tash was the first to mount her camel, which had obediently knelt down making it easier to climb on its back, legs folded up under its belly. Once Tash was aboard, the camel's handler said the magic words, and the camel raised itself, tipping Tash forward, but having listened to the handler she was expecting this and held firmly onto the pommels or saddle horns built into the saddle designed to make riding a safe experience.

Fluke was stood next to Tash's camel and looked up at Tash, now several feet higher than the top of Fluke's head.

Looking down she said, 'Your turn Fluke, c'mon it's easy, and very comfy!' She studied her saddle; it was made from a lightweight wooden frame and covered in multi coloured blankets and long tassels. Each saddle blanket was decorated slightly differently.

Fluke mounted his bull camel, but as he hadn't listened properly to its handler, he wasn't expecting the sudden movement when the dromedary lurched to its feet. He panicked as he was thrown forward, very nearly falling off the front, paws scrabbling around trying to find something to hang onto and with more luck than judgment he found the pommels at the front of his saddle, and he managed to stay on-board and regain his composure, hoping nobody had noticed.

'Up high, aren't we?' said Fluke gazing down to the sandy floor several feet below.

'At least you'll have a nice soft landing when you fall off Fluke...' laughed Tash, 'cos you're bound to have an accident sometime very soon!'

Fluke didn't have time to come back with a witty reply. The camel handlers moved all the racers to the start line. Twenty camels were milling around ready for the race to start. It had been agreed earlier there would be four laps of the track and the camels with their riders were eager to get started.

Tash looked at the throng of people below, hundreds of them, and noticed Salatis, Baba, Ishpi and Nebitka, along with several of the Nummers, all shouting words of encouragement and last minute words of wisdom, advice such as *hang on tight, don't get bunched in,* and *keep close to the inside line of the track.* She looked round to see how Fluke was faring; *badly* was the word that sprang to mind thought Tash. His camel was facing the wrong way, he'd somehow managed to steer his mount a complete 180 degree turn and he seemed to have little or no control over his animal.

Hang on tight...

'Use you reins Fluke...' she shouted over the cacophony of noise, 'turn its head around' but to no avail; Fluke's camel was a stubborn beast, very headstrong and didn't take too kindly to Fluke's requests. He tried pulling one rein, then the other, then he shouted at it, but no amount of rein pulling or shouting seemed to work, if anything it made his camel even more determined than ever to ignore its rider.

Fluke didn't know how the race was started, but it was, and he heard from behind him a mass stampede as all the camels – well, all the camels except his – start the race. So a herd of camels was belting around the track going one way, while Fluke's camel, startled by the sudden noise, shot off in the opposite direction. How he hung on was beyond him, the ungainly motion increased in intensity as his mount picked up speed and loped around the track.

Tash had positioned her camel next to the race favourite, a young lad from Deir-el-Medina, who was a good friend of Baba's. His camel swept immediately to the front of the pack, Tash was in second place as they headed into the first bend and made sure she kept her camel to the inside line. She could hear the rest of the camels close behind keeping up the frantic pace, she was sure she could feel the hot breath from the camels as they seemed that close, each camel and its rider desperate to win the race. Most of the riders came from local villages, and there was a lot of competition amongst the local communities. No money was at stake, just local bragging rights. Deir-el-Medina had won the race for the last three years and were yet again favourites to win.

Fluke had given up trying to steer his camel, he was more interested in just hanging on, and not as Tash had joked, be dumped from his ride into the soft sand several feet below. He managed a quick glance up ahead and noticed in horror a solid wall of approaching camels heading his way. His camel was fast, there was no denying it, keeping the same speed as all the others, so when they eventually met head on they were back near the start line. Ishpi and Salatis winced at the prospect of the potential collision.

Thankfully for everyone, the wall of approaching camels parted, allowing Fluke's camel an escape route, straight through the middle; an audible gasp from the watching spectators could be heard as the camels passed in opposite directions, then came sighs of relief as nobody collided.

Tash managed to shout over to Fluke as they passed each other, 'Next lap Fluke, try and slow down and jump onto my camel.' She wasn't sure if Fluke had understood, but she would find out on the next lap when they passed each other again.

She was still in second place, and had managed to open up a small gap from the chasing pack; *these camels are fast* she thought to herself, trying to keep up with the leader.

She was well into her second lap and looked up to see where Fluke was. He was getting closer by the second and Tash manoeuvred her camel away from the inside line, attempting to line up with the fast approaching Fluke. She noticed he was stood up in the saddle preparing himself for the dangerous jump from one camel to the other. Tash slowed as much as she could, but Fluke's camel had no intention of slowing down so this could be tricky. As they passed by, Fluke let go of the pommel, he'd already dropped the reins on the first lap as they didn't seem to make any difference, and leapt safely onto the back of Tash's camel.

'Are you ok Fluke?' Tash asked, concern evident in her voice.

'Phew, making that jump was something straight from a James Bond movie,' said a relieved Fluke, clinging onto the pommel at the back of Tash's saddle.

The exchange of riders meant the chasing pack had all but caught up, causing Tash to drop from second to fourth. With Fluke now safely on-board, albeit facing the wrong way, Tash spurred her camel on, desperate to reclaim second spot. As it turned out, it was quite handy Fluke was facing the wrong way: camels don't have wing mirrors, so Tash couldn't see how close the chasing pack was, and relied heavily on Fluke to let her know what was happening behind them.

Fluke passed on such words of wisdom as *speed up slow coach they're gaining on us!* He was doing everything he could think off to try and distract the riders behind him, anything to prevent them from closing the gap. They entered the fourth and final lap, Tash and Fluke had made up a lot of ground, and just as they crossed the finishing line they had clawed back some ground, enough to finish in a very respectable third position.

They all gathered back in the makeshift camel enclosure. The Bedouin tribesmen had taken the reins off their mounts and steered them back safely. Once the camels had knelt down, Fluke and Tash jumped off and were met with a whole lot of paw shaking and back slapping from Salatis, Baba and Ishpi.

'Well you two certainly have hidden talents...' Ishpi said proudly, 'first stonemasonry, then painters and decorators and now jockeys!'

Baba, beaming from ear to ear, put his arms around Fluke and Tash, 'I hope you enjoyed your surprise of the camel ride, you did say you wanted a go on a camel!'

'We certainly did Baba, thank you so much for organising this, it was exhilarating!' said a breathless Tash.

'One of the best fun things I've ever done...' confirmed Fluke, 'even if I couldn't steer properly. I don't think my camel liked me much as it didn't listen to any of my instructions!'

'I agree Fluke...' said Salatis, 'your camel was a stubborn beast, very headstrong, but the main thing is you got round in one piece, even if you did have to change camels halfway round! That was a pretty impressive leap from one camel to the other.'

The evening drew to a close, people headed back to their tents for an early night. Tomorrow was going to be a big day: most would be back at work, but Fluke and Tash were heading off to the city of Pi-Ramesses with Kahma.

'Can't wait for the morning Tash...' Fluke yawned, the day's excitement catching up with him, 'just glad the trip on our magic case will only take a few seconds as I'm not sure I could sit down too long, those saddles looked comfy but I think I've got saddle sore from all that riding!' And with his eyelids feeling very heavy he fell fast asleep.

Pi-Ramesses and the flying chariot...

Kahma was waiting patiently for them back at Salatis's house. Abana had made a hearty breakfast, and as usual the dining table was groaning under the weight of food. She had taken the liberty of inviting over Nedjem and her mother Tiaa as well. Abana knew that Baba would want to go along to Pi-Ramesses, and as much as she didn't want her son to go, she wasn't going to stop him from joining the adventure with his two new friends.

Abana had discussed Baba's trip in some depth with Salatis, and he had agreed it would do Baba the power of good to go to the city, it would be an education for his son and Kahma had agreed to look after Baba. She knew her son would miss Nedjem for a few days and thought it would be nice for them all to share breakfast and have a large family get-together.

'You must eat before your long journey to Pi-Ramesses,' she instructed Fluke, Tash and Baba. Fluke, not wanting to appear rude and upset his hosts, tucked in with gusto, chomping his way through the feast laid out before him.

Baba stopped shovelling food into his mouth and looked up at his mother with a confused look on his face. 'You mean that I can go along as well?' A big grin spread over his face, 'I wasn't even going to ask as I thought the answer would be no!'

Salatis put his hand on his son's shoulder, 'Kahma has agreed to look after all three of you, besides it's all part of growing up, mind you, it's not just going to be a few days' holiday my boy, I do actually want you to learn something whilst you're there!'

Tash meanwhile had finished her plate of food and went to their room, dragged out the magic case, which stood waiting patiently for its next passengers.

'We've never had four people on-board in one go...' said Tash, 'but if we huddle together there should be enough room!' They all took their positions and sat astride the magic case. It was a tight fit, but eventually they got comfortable and Tash double checked the settings and set the controls.

A chorus of *farewells* and *good lucks* was said by everyone stood watching, and they all gasped in amazement as Tash turned the handle three times, the gears engaged themselves, the case spun round and disappeared from sight, leaving an empty space where it had stood only seconds ago.

The four travellers hung on, especially Baba and Kahma, this was a completely new experience for them both, neither had flown before and the experience was both exhilarating and frightening in equal measure.

'Just don't look down!' were the words of wisdom shared by Fluke, his ears flapping in the wind, clearly enjoying himself. Baba had his eyes firmly shut, but Kahma, being an engineer and always curious, was looking in awe at the mile upon mile of desert spread out below.

Within seconds, Kahma, who was looking down over the edge of the case, could clearly see the massive city of Pi-Ramesses spread out before them. Tash made a good landing, the case only hopped, skipped and jumped a couple of times as they came to rest in a large square where ornamental stonework surrounded them and huge stone pillars supported impressive looking structures.

As they climbed off the case, Baba's eyes were now wide open. The shock of the last few seconds had rendered him near speechless, when eventually words began to tumble out of his mouth.

'How...? What just...? Did we...?' He didn't know what he really wanted to say, as he couldn't string together a complete coherent sentence.

Kahma stood back and admired the magic case, patting it with affection.

'I've got to get one of these!' he exclaimed, clearly impressed.

'It's one of a kind…' said Tash, 'trust me, there isn't another one like it!'

'Well you better look after it then…' grinned Kahma. 'C'mon everyone, follow me, we'd better head off to my workshop.' They all followed Kahma out of the square, with Baba and Tash at the rear dragging the case between them.

'The city looks huge,' said Fluke, walking alongside Kahma.

'It is Fluke – at the last estimate, we had a population of over 300,000 people living and working here. The city is spread over an area of roughly seven square miles…' Kahma confirmed. 'In the centre of the city where we just landed you have a huge central temple, with the grand palace of Ramesses II taking centre stage; to the west, alongside the river, you have a suburb of huge mansions built by the rich and wealthy which overlook the river, and to the east, where we are heading, there is an area of residential dwellings and workshops.'

They passed several people who knew Kahma, greetings were exchanged and one of the passers-by, Sipair, had a puzzled expression on his face.

'Hi Kahma, I thought you had several days off, a break from the daily grind and visiting family back in your home village?'

'I did Sipair, but I've cut my break short to come back in – we have a couple of new apprentices that need showing the ropes!' He grinned as he pointed to Fluke and Tash.

'Well you got back quickly, it takes me several days by camel – how did you manage it so fast?' The newcomer was eyeing the magic case suspiciously.

'You wouldn't believe me if I told you!' Kahma said casting a furtive glance at the magic case that was partially hidden from view by Tash and Baba, quickly ushering everybody off, walking rapidly in the direction of his workshop.

Tash and Fluke caught up with Kahma, 'You don't want anybody to know about our case then?' whispered Tash, picking up on Kahma's cautious comments to Sipair, glancing around to check if anybody was eavesdropping.

'Not really Tash – what with the war going on against the Hittite army, things are a bit tense around here. It pains me to say it Tash, but there may be spies amongst us, you just can't be too careful. Your case would be very valuable if it was stolen and fell into the wrong hands, and you'd be stranded here as well!'

Fluke shuddered at the last comment. The thought had never crossed his mind that they would be left stranded anywhere and he resolved to guard the case with his life.

Tash noticed the area they were now entering was not quite as glamorous as the square they had just left behind – it was, as described by Kahma, more industrial and contained smaller dwellings which were homes to the general workforce rather than the grand palatial royal palace where they had first landed. Kahma eventually led them into his workshops, which were much bigger than Tash thought they would be.

'Phew...' she whistled, 'when you said workshop, I pictured a tiny garage with a workbench, not this huge area. I thought it would be like Dad's garden shed back home – one small adjustable workbench, an assortment of mismatched screws in a tin, a bag of rusty nails, a hammer, a blunt drill, one spanner and a half set of screwdrivers.'

A seemingly endless line of workbenches disappeared into the depths of the massive hangar-like room. Each bench had several workers performing a different task from that of their neighbour.

'It's an assembly line...' said Kahma, turning to speak to Baba, Fluke and Tash. 'Once a section of the chariot is finished it's then moved on and over to the next bench for a new stage to be completed;

basically, construction is started one end of the line and by the time it reaches the end bench we have a completed war chariot.'

Baba was taking notes, scribbling away and drawing sketches on some papyrus parchment he had brought with him. 'Got to do some homework...' he said looking at Fluke and Tash peering over his shoulder. 'Dad will be checking my work when we get home!' he laughed.

Kahma's house...

The small group walked the full length of the production line, stopping occasionally to speak to the craftsmen busying themselves, who Tash noted were completely engrossed in their work.

'At the moment we're mainly carrying out repairs and constructing some urgent reserve chariots...' said Kahma. 'All of our chariots are on their way to the front line now, with our beloved Pharaoh Ramesses II preparing to go into battle,' he concluded, steering them all to a new large room located at the rear of the workshop.

'So what's in here?' asked Fluke.

'This is the foundry Fluke,' Kahma said, studying the awe on Baba's face as he admired the assembled furnace equipment, who was busily sketching the layout for his homework project set by Salatis. The furnaces currently stood idle, waiting for the next shift of workers. 'It gets very hot and bright in here when the furnace is lit. Maybe we'll come back in the morning when they fire up the furnace, but it's hot and dangerous so we might give it a miss, it just depends if we have time. First, I'll take you to my living quarters where you can freshen up, leave your belongings, and then we can head back here so you can get your hands dirty and help to build a chariot! A new shift of workers is due to start in an hour or so and I'll introduce you to a good friend who will look after you for the day.' They followed Kahma out of the workshop area and headed for the house he was using whilst he was stationed at Pi-Ramesses.

The accommodation was fairly large, nicely laid out and looked comfortable. There was a basic living area and a separate kitchen leading off from the main room and the dwelling had three bedrooms.

Fluke, Tash and Baba were sharing a room and they left the magic case carefully hidden under one of the beds. Baba took with him his papyrus notebook and pens, and Tash noted that Baba had already filled one whole page; he'd sketched out the layout of the workshop and drawn the equipment used in the furnace room.

Once they'd freshened up and changed clothes into old work gear, they headed back to the workshop. Kahma introduced the trio to one of his most trusted friends. 'Addaya, if you can spare a moment?' Kahma smiled and beckoned.

Addaya walked over and shook hands with Kahma. 'Oh, so you're back already! You obviously love it here so much my friend...' Addaya smiled a warm greeting and eyed the three newcomers. Introductions were made, and Addaya continued, 'You just can't keep away from the place can you? I thought you were starting your holiday? Two weeks of rest and relaxation you said, trips on the river with your lovely wife and best friend Paneferher, you boasted!' Addaya was kidding but Kahma took it all in his stride.

'Well, I needed to come back and keep an eye on you, can't have you slacking just because we finished the 2,000 war chariots for the great battle!'

Addaya laughed, but then a slightly serious look was etched on his face. He steered Kahma to one side and whispered, 'Word has quickly spread Kahma. Some people are talking about some mythical, magical chariot that you've used to get back here so quickly. Apparently the chariot has wings and soars through the air like a great bird? What is this wondrous piece of equipment? Some new design you've created and not told me about?'

Kahma looked at his friend's concerned face, his brow furrowed. 'It's nothing Addaya, people are mistaken. I mean really, *a flying chariot*? I'm good Addaya, but not that good – nobody except birds and gods can fly!' As much as Kahma tried to deny any knowledge of the magic case, he could feel his cheeks turning red, he was never any good at hiding secrets.

'Sipair said he spoke to you in the square – he's told everybody he saw you and three others flying on this great winged chariot that appeared out of nowhere. I don't trust that man Kahma, there's something shifty about him, always prying and sticking his nose in where he's not wanted.'

'He's a story teller, that Sipair. You know what he's like, he's been known to spin the odd tale, you should know better!' But Kahma was feeling uneasy, word had spread about the magic case, the flying chariot – they would have to tread carefully and play down these rumours.

Hastily changing the subject, Kahma asked Addaya if he could look after Fluke, Tash and Baba and show them around. Not only was Addaya a good friend of Kahma, he was also Ramesses's top military advisor and weapons trainer. He would be heading off to the front line within the next couple of days and was tying up a few loose ends before he left.

'Of course, it'll be my pleasure. I'll have these three working a shift repairing and building some new chariots, then I'll give them some weapons training, and I'll see if we can find some body armour to fit them, it will make the training really authentic. I'm leaving the day after tomorrow with extra provisions, more chariots, extra weapons and more infantry soldiers. Ramesses will need me on the front line with him. It's going to take a month of hard marching to catch up with the bulk of our army, and then, well, who knows the outcome of the war? Hopefully we can beat the Hittite army, but they are strong and well prepared.'

'A month...?' queried Fluke, 'won't the battle have started by then?'

'Who knows, Fluke?' It's a long march, through Egypt and over the border. Ramesses can be impatient, something we discussed before he left. He hadn't originally planned on starting his campaign until all his forces were in place, but he does like to recce the area first, that's why he's left early, but if the Hittites catch us by surprise...' His voice trailed off, not wanting to think of what the outcome could be. Nobody liked war, but the thought of letting the Hittites win and claim victory and move ever closer towards the Egyptian border was worrying everybody.

Hot water...

Addaya clapped his hands together, 'Enough of this war talk...' a broad smile returning to his face. 'That's for the future, let's get back to the more important issue of getting you three to work to earn your keep,' and he led Fluke, Tash and Baba over to the first work station.

'Can't believe we're actually going to make a war chariot Tash...' said Fluke excitedly, rubbing his paws together, eager to get started. 'Never had a go at carpentry before,' he continued as he took his place behind the workbench.

'I just hope your woodwork is better than your painting,' Tash laughed, remembering Fluke's stick man painting, and stood beside Fluke. Looking up she saw Baba, papyrus scroll in his hands, his pen fairly flying across the parchment as he drew rough sketches of Fluke and Tash at work.

'Will you be joining us Baba, or are you going to spend all day writing and drawing?' questioned Tash, slightly mischievously, sensing that Baba wasn't one for getting his hands dirty.

'Me? Manual labour...?' laughed Baba, 'I've got to keep an accurate record of events for Dad. *No slacking my boy* were his words.' said Baba, mimicking his Dad's parting comments before they left, 'so as much as I would like to get stuck in and help, I'm afraid I would be in the way, you two just carry on and pretend I'm not here.' And he continued his sketching.

All the workers seemed glad for a slight change in their working day. They were a proud workforce and always eager to show off their skills.

Fluke and Tash's first task was to construct the chariot wheels. They learnt that different types of cut timber were used for the various parts of the chariot: the wheel rims and spokes were made from imported elm; ash was used to construct the axles, and sycamore was used for the footboards.

'This is going to be a really silly question...' said Tash hesitantly to her tutor, a wheelwright. 'But how do you get the wood into a round shape? I mean you can't have square wheels can you?'

'Hot water Tash!' said her mentor.

'Yeah, which is exactly what we'll be in if this doesn't go right!' joked Fluke, eavesdropping.

'What do you mean hot water?' said Tash, ignoring Fluke's sarcastic comment.

'Two pieces of wood are used to make a wheel Tash, because the outer rim of the wheel is made up of two half circles joined together. They are cut to the right length, and left to soak in boiling hot water for several hours. When we think it's soaked long enough, we can bend it into a curved, half round shape. We insert the hot soaked wood between these sets of upright poles fixed securely into the ground...' he indicated a set of three poles, evenly spaced on the floor in an arc near his workbench. 'The wood is then held firmly in position until it cools down, and the wood retains its half-circle shape.'

'Crikey, that's pretty smart thinking,' Tash said, 'and the spokes of the wheel are made in a similar way?' Tash was suddenly distracted as she caught a glimpse of Fluke out of the corner of her eye, who was struggling with some hot wood that had just been removed from the boiling water.

'Ow! Ouch! Hot, hot hot...!' exclaimed Fluke, trying unsuccessfully to juggle the scalding piece of wood. 'That's soooo painful! I've burnt my paws, *again!*' he whined, clearly in discomfort, remembering his encounter with the hot sand when they first arrived.

'Yes, and don't forget the incident with the mallet either...' chuckled Tash, 'you and your paws, you need to be more careful!'

Tash and their wheelwright helped Fluke manhandle the hot pieces of timber by feeding them through the upright poles fixed securely in the ground, and began bending the timber as they fed it through the next set of poles, and noted with pride they had successfully formed the required half-circle.

'Easy!' said Fluke blowing on his hot paws trying to cool them down.

'We'll let these ones cool down a bit before we join them together,' said the wheelwright with a grin etched on his face. 'Onto the next section then – some that were prepared earlier are now ready to be joined together,' and reaching behind, he bent down and retrieved two half sections that had already been shaped and placed them on the workbench.

The assembly work was a lengthy process – the two halves were joined together, spokes were fitted to the centre hub and rim and securely tied with wet cattle intestines which hardened when they dried out; to complete the wheel, tyres made from rawhide were fitted to the outer rim.

'Wow – we've just made our first chariot wheel Fluke!' said Tash, the pride evident in her voice, as they stood back to admire their handiwork.

The rest of the day was spent moving down the production line; their wheel was taken to the next bench and they helped fit it to the axle and chassis, then the footboards were fitted and finally a completed chariot stood proudly, awaiting a final inspection from Addaya.

'Fantastic job...' said Addaya, 'the wheels look perfectly round to me, and the chassis looks sturdy. I think it's ready to be taken to the front as a reserve – Ramesses may need it as back up if any of the other chariots get damaged during the forthcoming battle.' With that he arranged for their chariot to be taken away and stored, ready for their long journey, catching up with Ramesses and his charioteer corps, the pride of the Egyptian military.

It had been a long, but hugely interesting day building war chariots, and eventually after they had helped clean up, there was a shift change and the night workers came into take over. Addaya whisked them out of the workshop and walked them back to Kahma's living quarters for dinner and agreed to meet them early in the morning for some combat training.

The traitor...

The narrow streets were an ominous place after sunset. Darkened alleyways housed some of the less than savoury residents of the city who resided here. Conditions were in complete contrast to the opposite side of the city where the rich lived in palatial residences and glamourous palaces that were in such abundance you could be forgiven to think all the city was wealthy. It wasn't.

A darkened figure scurried down one such narrow side street, occasionally stopping in a doorway and glancing back, checking to see if they had been followed, or maybe just out of habit to see where the next potential mugging may come from. Convinced they were alone and with no chance of any immediate danger, the figure continued its rat like scurrying, disappearing around a corner, and carried on to a rundown dwelling midway down the street. Pausing to check no one was following, they turned their attention to the doorway.

Tapping three short wraps with worn and calloused hands on the wooden door, the shadowy figure waited patiently until the door was opened slightly. Nobody officially lived here, the place was empty and used as a meeting point where secrets were exchanged for gold and silver currency in the form of jewellery.

The interior of the dwelling was as dark as the surrounding streets and any internal lights had been extinguished long before the approach of the furtive looking figure. A brief and whispered conversation took place. A rolled up parchment was withdrawn from an inside pocket and passed through the gap in the doorway, with an exchange of gold currency passed back. The furtive figure didn't wait around to check the amount of gold received, not wishing to hang around too long, as danger lurked around every corner. The figure scurried off, back the way they had come and the door closed firmly.

Several minutes passed before the door was opened again. The cloaked figure that appeared checked down both sides of the street, happy in the knowledge that his ill-gotten gains would be rewarded handsomely by the Hittite army lead by King Muwatalli. The unrecognisable figure scampered off in the opposite direction to his counterpart, heading back to his normal part of the city, back home to the wealth he had grown accustomed to, and secure in the knowledge that the information he had obtained would keep him in considerable wealth for a very long time.

Military school...

Addaya met them at Kahma's the next morning, and bright sunshine greeted them as they made their way over to the military training school. The pride of the Egyptian army were trained here – charioteers, foot soldiers, archers and swordsmen.

A new class was about to start and Tash asked Addaya if they could join in with the training.

'Of course you can Tash, I'll have my soldiers take it easy with you as it's your first time. I just hope you won't be out of your depth too much.'

'First time...?' Fluke laughed, 'We've just rescued Marion from the castle, battled the evil Sheriff and taught his soldiers a lesson they won't forget! We've been trained by none other than the great Robin Hood!' said Fluke, but was hushed by Tash.

'Let it be a surprise to them Fluke, they won't be expecting us to be any good!' Tash whispered, grinning mischievously, to which Fluke nodded his approval.

'They won't know what's hit them Tash...' he sniggered, whispering behind his paw so Addaya couldn't hear. 'I take it you remember everything we've been taught?'

'Oh yeah...!' she replied with glee, 'let's get started!' eager to show the Egyptians they weren't the only ones with military training.

They were led into the armoury where Tash and Fluke busied themselves sifting through scale armour costumes, the standard battle dress of the Egyptian army, and eventually found some that fitted.

Fully suited, they studied each other closely to make sure the costumes were on properly.

'Well, don't we look the business,' said Fluke with a grin, 'we've certainly worn some different costumes on our last couple of adventures!' he chuckled.

They made their way out onto the busy parade ground to meet up with Addaya, who was busy organising his troops into small groups for training sessions. Some were fighting with swords, others were practising defensive techniques using small round leather looking shields, and another group, way off in the distance, was honing up on their archery skills. The archers were stood on makeshift platforms that closely resembled the footboards of a chariot, balanced precariously on timber logs, which were being rocked back and forth by troops that stood either side. They were trying to re-create the motion they would feel if the chariot was in full flight over rough ground; these well trained archers didn't have the luxury of firing their arrows whilst stationary, the battle was always carried out at full speed over rough terrain.

'Well don't you two look the part...?' said Addaya to Fluke and Tash. 'Come and join in some sword work and we'll see how you get on.'

Tash took up her position as her training from Robin Hood, Little John and the rest came flooding back. The soldier she confronted was massive, and attired in the same scale armour costume as Tash, his sword at the ready. She heard Addaya whisper to the soldier *take it easy on the new recruit*. Well, Tash flew into action, and re-enacted the battle on the log with Little John, her sword flashed brightly in the sunshine, causing her would-be assailant to stagger back from the onslaught, desperately trying to regain some composure and not be completely outclassed by a cat – she might look like Bastet, the cat goddess, but she was only a cat.

Shamefaced that he had been beaten by Tash, the soldier skulked off to the next training group, hoping that none of his colleagues had witnessed the spectacle.

Addaya, open-mouthed and dumbstruck eventually managed to utter some words. 'I can't believe what I've just witnessed – you've just beaten, well no, thrashed one of our top soldiers, Tash. How, may I ask, did you manage that display? Your technique was excellent! Who's trained you both?'

Fluke had also despatched his soldier with ease, sending him away equally shamefaced, much to his colleague's delight, knowing he wasn't the only soldier to be thrashed by a new recruit.

'Robin Hood – he's the one who trained us,' said Tash, wistfully remembering their recent adventure back in Sherwood.

'Never heard of him,' said Addaya rubbing his chin, deep in thought, 'is he local? If he is, why haven't I heard his name mentioned.'

'Err no... he's definitely not local!' said Fluke, standing beside Tash, 'in fact, I can say with some certainty, he's not even been born yet!'

Addaya looked confused, but Fluke carried on speaking, 'Don't ask, Addaya, trust me, it's too complicated to explain!' Fluke had a grin that spread from ear to ear, and the pair moved off chuckling to each other and headed towards the archery school.

Carrier pigeons...

*A*rchery training was going well. The rocking motion of the platform and logs, designed to replicate actual battle conditions, took some getting used to, but they were soon accustomed to the new sensation, and it was reassuring to see their archery skills were as good as ever. Fluke whispered to Tash to *slow down a bit and take it easy*, as they didn't want to embarrass the rest of the soldiers too much.

As a barrage of arrows flew towards their targets far off in the distance, Tash looked up and noticed a loan carrier pigeon circling overhead, eventually flying off towards its loft. She didn't think too much about it, and waited patiently for another turn on the platform. She stepped up and strung an arrow into her bow, arm pulled back waiting to release the arrow towards its intended target, when out of nowhere she heard a shout and noticed a figure rushing over, waving a small piece of parchment, frantically trying to get the attention of Addaya.

The figure was Kahma, and he stopped short, clearly out of breath, a worried look etched on his face.

'Slow down Kahma,' said Addaya, 'what can be so urgent that it makes *you* of all people run!' He tried to joke with his best friend, but suddenly realised whatever news Kahma had to tell him wasn't in the least bit funny and must be serious.

Bent over double, hands resting on his thighs, breathing in great lungfuls of fresh air and trying to calm himself sufficiently to get his words out, Kahma eventually managed to say, 'It's Ramesses! He's in serious trouble. One of his best carrier pigeons has just delivered this note directly from the front line. It appears that two captured Hittite spies had led Ramesses to believe the Hittite army was at least 200km away from Kadesh in the land of Aleppo, a long way off, but it turns out it was a lie, the whole Hittite army and several of their allies are waiting to ambush Ramesses. He's been too eager to get to Kadesh, his four Divisions are spread miles apart. King Muwatalli has many allies and countries supporting him – some estimate up to 19 different allies are fighting alongside him, with many thousands of troops, the last estimate is up to 50,000 and a far greater number of chariots, somewhere in excess of 4,000. What does Ramesses have? Last count was 2,000 chariots and 20,000 troops, and these are all spread apart, oh I fear the worst Addaya, I really do.'

The archery contest had ground to a halt. Everybody stood open-mouthed as they digested this distressing piece of bad news.

Addaya put his hand up to stop Kahma, paused briefly and said calmly, 'Well, we have no option, I must leave immediately for Kadesh. It may take a month of hard marching, but if Ramesses can hold out that long we may be in time.'

'One man isn't going to make a difference Addaya,' said Kahma, the panic evident in his voice.

'No, agreed, but I'm his military advisor, master tactician and good friend, I can't stay here and do nothing!' he exclaimed, his mind calmly trying to sort out what to do first.

'You'll never make it in time, one month is a long time!' Kahma confirmed what all the archers must be thinking.

Tash shared a knowing look with Fluke. Tash politely coughed and interrupted. 'Err, Addaya, you know that flying chariot Sipair thought he saw earlier? Well, it does exist, and we can get you to the front in a matter of seconds, can't we, Kahma?'

Hope suddenly spread over Kahma's face and a smile replaced the previous frown.

'Of course! How silly of me. Tash is right: Addaya, we can have you there in a matter of seconds! The story of the flying chariot is true.'

'I knew you were hiding something...' Addaya grinned, 'why didn't you tell me about your new design?'

'It's not my design, although I wish I could take credit for it! It's Tash and Fluke's chariot – I only found out it existed a short while ago, and we came back from Deir-el-Medina in a matter of seconds. The case is back at my house – c'mon, let's go!'

They hurried off, an added urgency and spring in their steps as Kahma led the way.

'Surely only the gods can have a flying chariot?' Addaya was finding it hard to believe such a miracle could really exist.

'Yes agreed, but who does she look like Addaya?' Kahma pointed to Tash.

Addaya studied Tash, then gasped when it suddenly dawned on him – 'Bastet! Of course! Our great cat goddess! Bastet has come to save the day! It's a sign, surely – divine intervention; help from the gods in our hour of need!'

Fluke slapped his paw against his forehead, 'Oh no, not this again,' he muttered to himself. 'Big head's head, just got bigger! Just remember Tash – if and when we get home, you're not going to keep going on about this are you? I never have been, or never will, be your servant! *Oh Fluke, bring me this will you* or *oh Fluke, would you carry that for me?*' He mimicked what he thought a royal cat goddess might sound like.

Lost luggage...

They made rapid progress, picking Baba up from the workshop on the way, all of them walking fast, nearly breaking into a run, although Fluke noted that Kahma probably wouldn't be able to run for a while, such were his poor fitness levels.

Their urgency was very apparent as they all tumbled through the main front door of Kahma's house. Fluke had explained to Baba along the way what had happened, bringing him up to date with the predicament that Ramesses faced.

Tash hastily made her way into the bedroom to collect the case, closely followed by Fluke. Tash stopped dead in her tracks, a look of shock and anguish on her face and barely noticed that Fluke had run into the back of her.

'Why have you stopped Tash, come on get the case out from under the bed...' His voice trailed off as he noticed with dismay what had caused Tash to suddenly stop.

The room was a mess and in complete disarray, furniture upended, clothes thrown everywhere, and the bed pulled away from the wall and turned upside down.

'Well that's that then Fluke,' said Tash, clearly upset, turning to Fluke, 'our worst nightmare has come true. We've been burgled, our case has been stolen – we're stranded here – we can't ever go home.'

A stunned silence filled the air, even Fluke, never one to be quiet, was speechless. Eventually he muttered, 'But who Tash...? Why...? How did they know what they were stealing?' Words were tumbling out of his mouth. 'You must be mistaken Tash, it's just got to be here somewhere!' although deep down he knew it was pretty clear their case had gone.

Kahma came into the room and surveyed the scene for himself. 'It's Sipair, it must be him! He's been acting really strange these last few days, and remember earlier today he was showing some unhealthy interest in your magic case Tash, spreading rumours about the flying chariot. I saw him hanging around outside my house earlier, and he left in a hurry several hours ago, his camels were laden with all his belongings, he told me he had some urgent business to attend to and would be gone for several days. I should have known better!'

'He doesn't understand what he's got though!' Tash said.

'Doesn't matter Tash, he knows it's magic therefore worth a lot of money to the highest bidder – I dare say he's going to try and sell it to Muwatalli – it could make him a rich man.'

'He doesn't know how to operate it. It could transport him anywhere, back or forwards in time! We must get it back soon or we're never likely see it again, and we'll be stranded here for good!'

Addaya, ever the calming influence, spoke up and took control of the situation. 'When did you say he left?' He directed his question to Kahma.

'A few hours ago,' Kahma confirmed, 'not long after you took Fluke and Tash into the military school. I came back here to collect some paperwork and noticed the little weasel hanging around outside, looking very shifty, but I never imagined in a thousand years that he would resort to theft.'

'You say he left by camel?' Addaya was thinking ahead, his tactical brain was calculating all the possibilities.

'Yes, but that was hours ago,' Kahma said.

'Fluke, Tash, I've heard you can race camels, now's the time to see if you can ride some of our Pharaoh's finest race horses. Camels are great over long distances but nowhere near as fast as the fine race horses we keep here. The horses that Ramesses has stabled here are swift and run like the wind. There's a chance, albeit it a slim chance, that we may be able to catch up with

Sipair before he gets out of range of our horses. Any chance, no matter how small has got to be worth a go, so let's get to the stables and saddle up, time is against us!'

Tash could see why Addaya was Ramesses's military advisor, calm under pressure and always thinking ahead, just like a good chess player, always planning several moves ahead, trying to out-think his opponent.

The chase...

The stable boys were thankfully alert, and in a matter of minutes had saddled up 11 of the Pharaoh's best race horses. Addya took Fluke, Tash and eight of his most trusted soldiers with him – all fully armed and ready to go. Baba asked if he could tag along; he wanted to be part of the adventure as well. It was agreed, although Baba couldn't ride a horse, he would sit behind and would ride with Addaya.

'It goes without saying that we've got to fly like the wind, but with luck and good fortune we'll catch up with Sipair. He doesn't know that we've discovered he's a traitor, knowing him like we all do, he'll be complacent and won't be in as much of a hurry as we are. Did he have any travelling companions with him Kahma?' Addaya was sat upright in his saddle looking down at his friend.

'A dozen men with him, not too many, but enough to put up a struggle if and when you catch up with them.'

Addaya snorted, 'Oh we'll catch him don't you worry, and as for Sipair putting up a struggle? He might be desperate to escape, but in all seriousness looking at the way Fluke and Tash have performed in training I think they could take on all of them and come out victorious, but we're not going to take any chances, we've got some back up!' He turned around in his saddle to look over his fully armed men, noting the gleam in their eyes – a look that comes when adrenalin was coursing through their bodies, eager to be off and give chase.

Eleven horses turned round and began to filter out of the stables.

'Be careful, and come back safely!' Kahma shouted up to Baba, Fluke and Tash as they all rode single file. Addaya and one of his soldiers, who was an expert tracker, led the way. Tash was next in line, closely followed by Fluke who was still trying to master his horse, holding onto his reins and attempting to look like he knew exactly what he was doing. His fine horse was oblivious to its jockey, it was just following the rest of the pack, picking up speed as they left the confines of the city, heading, they hoped, to catch up with Sipair and the magic case.

The horses broke into a gallop with Fluke successfully hanging on, just, and eventually beginning to master his mount. The horses were throwing up a mini sandstorm in their wake. Thankfully the riders were all wearing long lengths of cloth wrapped round their faces to stop them from swallowing mouthfuls of dust and sand. All were focused on making up ground on their target.

Two hours of fast riding and Addaya reined in his horse, the following pack slowed and they all dismounted for a few minutes to give the horses a rest. Everybody took out their water carriers and drank heartily. The group gathered around Addaya's chief scout who was bent down, kneeling in the sand carefully studying camel tracks. A brief exchange of words passed between the scout and Addaya, who turned around and said, 'We're on the right course, these tracks are fresh and camels have passed through here very recently.'

'How do you know they're fresh?' asked Fluke, kneeling down next to a long line of prints in the sand, carefully studying each hoof print, trying to determine how the tracker knew they were fresh tracks.

'Well, there's no real way of telling Fluke, but the big pile of camel dung you've nearly knelt in is very fresh!' And everybody laughed as Fluke suddenly realised what the funny smell was, glancing down he was inches away from the pile of dung. The bright sun had partially dazzled him, causing him to miss it, but luckily his sense of smell was ok.

The horses, now partially rested and watered, were champing at the bit, raring to go, picking up the urgent vibes from the group. Everyone mounted their trusty horses and headed off in haste, desperate to close the gap, capture the spy Sipair, and hopefully retrieve their magic suitcase.

Another half hour of intense riding followed. They galloped up a steep mound and reaching the summit Addaya slowed his mount, everybody followed suit and waited patiently. Scanning the horizon they all witnessed in the distance a small sandstorm.

'We've found you Sipair, you traitor!' Addaya shouted in triumph. Turning around in his saddle he said to his men, 'I know your horses must be tiring but our enemy is in sight, so in the name of Ramesses let's finish this now!' Urging his men onwards, and making sure Baba was holding on tight, the 11 horses raced down the mound, reached the flat plain and rapidly made up the short distance on their quarry.

With Sipair now in plain sight, Tash let out an ear splitting '*Chaaaaarge!*' causing Baba and Fluke to jump out of their skins.

'Crikey Tash, you scared me and I know you. Lord only knows what Sipair and his men must be thinking!' Fluke hollered back to Tash, desperately trying to make himself heard over the din their horses were making. Addaya and the rest of his men followed suit, shouting out their own battle cries as they made contact at long last. Eleven horses surrounded the dozen camels, forming a loose perimeter ring around them. Addaya, his men, Fluke and Tash all dismounted, Baba had been positioned out of harm's way by Addaya, the last thing he wanted was any harm coming to his good friend Salatis's son and heir. Sipair and his followers also dismounted from their camels and a brief stand-off ensued.

'Sipair, you're a traitor, you've stolen the magic chariot and were heading to sell it, along with other secrets I no doubt, to Ramesses's greatest enemy – Muwatalli. You'll be brought back to Pi-Ramesses to face trial.'

Sipair's face showed touches of panic, but he defiantly stood his ground. 'Never! You'll never get me back to that city, Ramesses is a doomed Pharaoh, the great King Muwatalli will crush Ramesses's army, and the Hittite Empire will sweep through Egypt and gain control of the whole region.'

'Not if we have anything to say in the matter,' Fluke glared angrily at Sipair.

Raising their swords, both Fluke and Tash lunged at Sipair, whose men had unsheathed their swords, preparing for a fight. It was evident, however, they didn't really have the heart for a battle – the reputation of Addaya and his well-trained soldiers was legendary. A brief exchange of intricate sword play by Fluke and Tash followed, but Sipair had had no military training – he had always thought himself well above that – and within a few seconds he dropped his sword in the sand and fell to his knees. Looking up at Addaya he begged for forgiveness. His followers all did the same, surrendering to Addaya's soldiers.

'I beg you, please don't hurt me! My head has been turned. Muwatalli has paid handsomely to install spies at the great city of Pi-Ramesses. I only did what I did for money, you must understand surely? Anybody in my position would do the same!'

Addaya glared angrily, 'Money? Never in a million years would any of us...' he indicated his men, 'contemplate treachery. You've had a good life so far Sipair, living a life of luxury in a grand city built by our beloved Pharaoh Ramesses, so I ask you – why would you want to betray our Pharaoh? For money you say? That makes it worse, you're weak, greedy and evil, a truly horrible combination. You and your men...' he looked disdainfully at the bedraggled line of Sipair's followers kneeling in the sand, 'will be brought back to the city to face trial. More importantly we will search your belongings to find out what secrets you were intending to sell.'

The stolen book...

Tash was the first to start searching, and she chose the closest camel, rummaging through the luggage and belongings. No magic suitcase was found, so she joined Fluke and Baba to go through the next camel's luggage. Again nothing was found and panic was beginning to creep in. *What if Sipair had already passed the magic case to another spy?*

They frantically searched the luggage on a few more camels until they came to the sixth, they were about to start a thorough search when they heard a cry of joy from Addaya who had started searching the furthest camel down the line.

'I take it this is the famed chariot?' he shouted down the line to Tash, who had stopped her search, looking up expectantly to witness Addaya holding the suitcase aloft proudly.

With relief, Tash and Fluke made their way over and gratefully retrieved their case, a huge grin was spread over Fluke's face now they were reunited with their flying chariot. Tash patted her case with affection, 'Oh it's good to have you back!' and began running her eyes over the case, checking for any signs of damage, but all looked in order. She opened the case to retrieve the book containing all the dates and co-ordinates. Fluke looked over at Tash, his grin slowly beginning to fade and disappearing completely when he noticed the agitated and concerned look on Tash's face as she delved deeper into the lining of the case – the booklet was missing.

'It's not here Fluke, the book's gone!' she said in dismay.

'Well look harder Tash, it's got to be there it just has to be!'

Tash handed over the case to Fluke, 'You have a look then!' and he duly delved as deep as he could, rummaging around, but came back with the same findings; the book was gone.

'Now what?' he turned to Tash, hoping against hope she had an answer.

She pondered the question and was about to reply when she noticed Addaya staring at Sipair. Addaya had noticed Sipair glancing over to one of his fellow traitors, who was currently being tied and trussed, and was ready to be put back on his camel, and had very nearly missed the exchange of eye contact between the pair.

'Hold on there.' He walked over to Sipair and did a body search, checking his pockets, and found on the inside of his tunic, the book, carefully secreted away.

'Even now you try to deceive us Sipair. Will you never learn your lesson?' He shook his head and handed the book over to Tash, who gratefully accepted the book and secured it back where it belongs, inside the suitcase.

Sipair, realising he was in a big heap of trouble, crumbled completely and gave Addaya the roll of parchment he had obtained, containing information he had intended to sell to Muwatalli, all of Ramesses's military tactics, troop numbers, the arms and equipment they had; if this report had fallen into enemy hands it would have been pivotal to the outcome of the pending war.

Addaya scanned the skyline and noted the night was drawing in. He surveyed the scene laid out before him. All of Sipair's followers were now bound securely and the small threat they had posed was nullified. Fluke could see Addaya visibly relax, now part of the job was complete, the spies were caught, Ramesses's military secrets hadn't made it to the enemy and, more importantly, as far as Fluke and Tash were concerned, their magic suitcase had been found.

'We'll make camp here tonight, and at first light Tash you'll have to show me how your magic chariot can fly us to be with Ramesses,' Addaya said and then turned to his trusty soldiers and continued, 'You will have to take the traitors back to the city for them to stand trial. Once these vermin have been dealt with, arrange for reinforcements to make a hasty trip back. Everything should be ready and in place as we were due to leave soon anyway. I know it will be a month of hard riding to get to the frontline, but as we don't know how long the battle with the Hittites will go on for, you may yet be in time to help.'

'Where will we sleep tonight?' Tash asked and turned to Addaya, 'I mean we left in a hurry and didn't pack anything for an overnight stopover in the desert.'

Addaya laughed and said, 'I'm sure Sipair won't mind us using his tents.' He glanced over at the bound and trussed figure. 'They have all the equipment we'll need here in their luggage, and it looks like they had packed enough provisions for a very long journey, which just confirms they never intended to return back home.'

Camp was made, tents erected quickly and a campfire started. Fluke and Tash learned the tents were a traditional Bedouin style. Made from woven goat and camel hair, they kept the desert wind out and stored the heat inside, as while the daytime heat of the desert was intensely hot, the opposite could be said for the nights: when the sun dipped below the horizon, desert nights were cold and unforgiving.

Fluke took charge of the food, dishing out a wonderful feast of stewed lamb, served on a bed of rice and flatbreads. He hadn't realised how hungry he was; wonderful aromas wafted around the camp and everybody tucked in with gusto. The horses were loosely tethered together, fed, watered and settled down for the night.

Plans for tomorrow's adventure were discussed in greater detail. Addaya sat round the campfire, with Baba, Fluke and Tash either side.

Tash looked over at Baba, who had been busy writing notes, and drawing sketches at every opportunity he had.

'You've been busy Baba,' Tash leaned over to see what was being written.

'It's my job Tash,' Baba said with a grin, his eyes never leaving the parchment paper, scribbling away intently, 'it's like a diary, jotting down what we've been up to so far on our adventure, I must say we've packed a lot into just a few days, I'm just happy that Dad let me come along, I've learnt a lot and it beats going to school!'

The conversations began to dwindle, Fluke yawned, which set everybody else yawning and it was agreed it was time for bed. It was going to be a big day tomorrow and rest was important. Tash and Fluke made sure the case was within reach, not wanting to let it out of their sight as they drifted off into a deep sleep.

Off to Kadesh...

They woke early and witnessed a spectacular sunrise. It really was a sight to behold, the bright orange orb just beginning to peek over the distant horizon, filling the landscape with its long fingered rays as they reached out, casting light, and banishing the night's darkness for a few hours and spreading warmth across the dunes.

They didn't have any breakfast as time was against them, so the tents and cooking utensils from last night's feast were packed up and stored with the other luggage on the camels, ready to head back to Pi-Ramesses.

Addaya was in discussions with his soldiers, giving them last minute instructions, making sure their cargo of traitors were firmly tied up, and ready to be shipped back to the city for trial. Addaya had tried to persuade Baba to go back to the city and out of danger, but the young scribe was having none of it. He wanted to go to Kadesh and finish his diary that he had been writing ever since he had started this exciting adventure.

Fluke, Tash and Baba stood side by side and watched the departing camel train move off. The camels, with their ungainly gait, walked off and disappeared over the nearest dune, leaving just the four of them with the magic case.

Tash took charge and retrieved the book from within the case, quickly finding the page she needed. Setting the co-ordinates for Kadesh, she got Fluke and Addaya to double check them as she didn't want to land right in the middle of a battle. Addaya had given Tash the last known co-ordinates to where Ramesses had made camp before releasing the carrier pigeons on their long flight back to the city. Satisfied she had entered the right destination co-ordinates they climbed aboard, Tash up-front, Fluke behind her, with Baba next and Addaya at the back. Four people was the maximum the case could hold and it was a bit of a tight squeeze, but they all managed to sit comfortably.

'Are you ready?' Tash turned around, noting with interest Addaya had his eyes firmly shut, and his knuckles had turned white as he clung to the side of the case. The thought of actually flying filled him with both dread and excitement. Baba meanwhile had an excited look etched on his young face; he had already experienced a trip on the case so knew what to expect and set about reassuring his elder.

'Don't worry Addaya, Tash is a good driver and we'll be there in a matter of seconds, think of it as an adventure, something to boast about to your children – *The great Addaya, flying into battle, side by side with Bastet, our great cat goddess.* Baba's calming words had the desired effect, Addaya visibly relaxed, smiled and thanked Baba.

'Well, what are we waiting for...?' Addaya said, his confidence returning, 'We've got our beloved Pharaoh to rescue!' and with that Tash turned the handle three times, the wind picked up, the magic suitcase started to spin, and promptly vanished into thin air. If anybody had been there to witness their departure, all they would have seen was a small sandstorm that the departing case had left behind.

Ramesses II...

Ramesses was again pacing up and down; the interrogation of the two captured spies had provided him with worrying news – the Hittites weren't at Aleppo as he had first been told. The whole of the Hittite army, along with several of Muwatalli's allies, were camped behind the old city of Kadesh. Ramesses knew he was severely outnumbered, his forces were stretched too far apart. He remonstrated with himself, he shouldn't have been so hasty. He had been too keen to recapture Kadesh and stop the advance of the Hittite army, led by his enemy Muwatalli, before he gained too much momentum. One of Ramesses's messengers ran into the tent, breathlessly, clutching a rolled up parchment.

'My lord Pharaoh...' He gasped for air, 'I bring news. One of your scouts, recently despatched with the order for the Divisions of Re, Ptah, Seth and Ne'arim to make haste, has returned and has just this minute ridden back into camp to bring desperate news.' He handed a parchment from the Re Division to Ramesses, bowed and backed out of the tent, leaving Ramesses to unroll the hastily written script. Looking over at his armed guards who stood to attention either side of the tent entrance, his brow was furrowed in concern. The news as feared was not good – dreadful would be a more accurate description. His nearest Division of Re, trailing his own Amun Division by several miles, had come under a surprise attack from the Hittites. He read through the message again, digesting the bad news. It would appear his Re Division had been decimated by the heavy Hittite chariots, which had literally smashed their way through the front ranks of the Re. Any remaining bedraggled troops were desperately trying to regroup to meet up with Ramesses and his Amun Division that were currently camped near Kadesh, close to the Orontes River.

Ramesses was about to leave his tent and make his way over to meet up with his commanders and generals when an aide burst through the tent flaps.

'It would appear something is heading our way Lord Pharaoh, and is approaching very fast,' the aide said, wringing his hands together nervously, bowing in awe to his great Pharaoh.

'Explain yourself, man,' commanded Ramesses, confused, as his aide normally provided accurate information and wasn't easily rattled.

'We don't know what it is…' the aide said truthfully, glancing over at the two armed guards.

'It's just a small speck on the horizon and is moving faster than anything we've ever seen. Whatever it is, it's surrounded by a sandstorm and is heading directly towards our camp. It may be a surprise attack by the Hittites? Shall I ready our men?'

'Let me see for myself,' Ramesses said calmly and was about to make his way out of the tent, the flaps held apart by his two guards, when the 'sandstorm' flew through the opening like a guided missile and came to an abrupt halt, crashing into the rear of the tent, which thankfully didn't collapse.

The two guards leapt into action and hovered over the new arrival, long spears held firmly and pointing menacingly at the heap on the floor, not really sure what to do. The sandstorm began to settle and Ramesses began to make out four figures, covered in sand and lying in a heap on the floor. Realisation dawned on Ramesses and a huge grin formed on his face.

'Put your spears away,' he instructed his two guards, 'we have a very welcome visitor.' Reaching down he offered Addaya a helping hand.

The four new visitors that had rather unceremoniously crashed through the tent got to their feet and paws respectively, and stood gazing around.

'Ramesses, you're still in one piece, so thankfully we're not too late...' Addaya grasped the offered outstretched hand of his Pharaoh and good friend, and gave a warm embrace in return. 'We received the message from the carrier pigeon and feared the worst. Thank the gods! If it hadn't been for Fluke and Tash here...' he indicated his travelling companions, 'we would still be a month of hard marching away.' Addaya released Ramesses's hand and went over to stand between Fluke, Tash and Baba. 'Three new recruits for you,' he said jokingly, 'although in all seriousness Fluke and Tash here will come in very handy in the heat of the battle as they certainly have the right skills, and young Baba here is the son and heir to Salatis.'

'I wondered why he looked familiar,' beamed Ramesses and shook his hand. 'If you take after your father, my new building projects and plans for future pyramid and city building will certainly be in good hands over the next few years. Now tell me more about our new friends.' He stepped over to Fluke and Tash, who both bowed respectively, knowing they were in the presence of a truly great Pharaoh.

Baba introduced Ramesses to Fluke and Tash and explained how they all met, describing in detail the magic case, to which Ramesses kept glancing at it in wonderment, pyramid building, painting, chariot building, camel racing and their adventure capturing Sipair. Ramesses shook his head sadly at the mention of a traitor in his city. Baba finally finished his story telling with what Fluke and Tash hoped to do before they went home.

Ramesses looked on in awe; as Pharoah, it wasn't very often he was rendered speechless, but after Baba had explained their adventures thoroughly, Ramesses looked over at Fluke, Tash and the magic case, a grin spread over his face. 'I think Muwatalli and his Hittite army could be in for a big surprise.' He instructed that they all sit down in a circle on a huge rug, the magic case in the middle the centre of attention, and immediately Addaya and Ramesses were planning and talking tactics.

Making plans...

Ramesses was a good host and it was obvious to Fluke, Tash and Baba they were privy to some serious tactical discussions. Ramesses's generals had all been summoned and room was made on the rug to accommodate the large gathering. The meeting went on for most of the morning and it was agreed by most present that a dawn assault on the Hittite ranks would be best, they would hope to catch them napping and hopefully the attack would be well under way before the enemy realised what was happening.

New messengers arrived throughout the morning with minute by minute updates on the positions of the Hittite army and their allies, and more importantly updates on when the rest of Ramesses's army Divisions would arrive to bolster his attacking force. They were getting closer but still some distance away. His Re Division that had been attacked, had managed to re-form themselves, albeit in a bedraggled formation, and were headed with as much haste as they could muster to the frontline to join up with Ramesses's Amun Division; the rest of his Divisions of Ptah,

Seth and Ne'arim were approaching from slightly different directions and were expected to arrive sometime the following afternoon at the latest.

The meeting was adjourned with everybody present now fully aware of what was expected of them. They were to hit the Hittites hard and fast; speed being crucial and as the new lightweight chariots were supremely fast and agile Ramesses hoped they could run rings around their foes. The generals marched off to organise their separate units and prepare themselves and troops for the dawn raid.

The tent emptied rapidly leaving Ramesses, Addaya, Fluke, Tash and Baba.

'So this flying chariot of yours...' Ramesses approached the case, a bewildered look etched on his face, 'is obviously fast, a whole lot faster than anything we currently have at our disposal. If you feel confident enough I would like you to be by my side tomorrow morning when we launch our counter attack.'

Fluke looked over to Tash, a grin spread on their faces at the prospect of fighting alongside Ramesses.

'Our magic case or, should we say, flying chariot, is at your disposal, and we'll be honoured to fight alongside you,' Tash said and continued, 'anything we can do to help would be a privilege.'

'It will be tough,' Addaya confirmed, 'the Hittites are no push-overs, they have a superb army, but I've seen you two in training and I believe you should be more than capable in holding your own, but this is the Egyptians' fight and we wouldn't expect you to get involved and join in, you've done more than your fair share already in just getting me here.'

'Involved? You try stopping us...' Fluke spoke up, 'it's what we're here for, call it our destiny but it's why we are here.'

Looking over to Baba, Addaya said, 'I think Baba that you should stay on the side lines taking tactical notes for your diary. Your dad wouldn't take too kindly or be too impressed if I took you into battle, you were only meant to go to Pi-Ramesses as an educational visit, not join in any fighting!'

Baba looked a bit crestfallen, but Tash noticed that secretly he wasn't too upset at not being invited to join in the battle.

'I guess you're right...' Baba said, slightly relieved. 'I've had no training, well nothing compared to Fluke and Tash here, trained by this Robin Hood person I've heard all about, and would probably just end up getting in the way.'

Ramesses smiled and put an arm around his pair of new friends. 'Thank you both, it is really appreciated, if only everybody was as loyal as you two,' obviously referring to the traitor Sipair which still left a bad taste in everybody's mouth.

Fluke and Tash were escorted out of the tent, and along with Addaya went over to the barracks where the main troops were stationed. Finding the tent which was used as the weapon store room, they were kitted out with body armour, bows, arrows, shields and anything else they could think off that may be of use. Fluke and Tash admired their new costumes, both sniggering as they looked each other up and down.

'What do you think Mum and Dad would think if they could see us now?' laughed Tash.

'They'd be in a state of shock I would imagine! They think we're still curled up on the sofa back in the bedroom, snoozing and being good quiet family pets!' Fluke grinned whilst adjusting his body armour to fit comfortably. Noticing a slingshot, a type of handheld catapult in the bottom of the huge box of weapons, he retrieved it, studied it carefully, and tucked it into his waistband. 'Might come in handy,' he muttered to himself.

Addaya took the three of them around the camp and introduced them to as many people in the allotted time they had left before nightfall. The sun seemed to set quite quickly, and with an early sunrise, the nights were short.

Word had spread around camp of the magical flying chariot, and both Fluke and Tash were treated with respect and treated as equals, an honour not normally bestowed on new recruits.

Addaya took them over to their sleeping accommodation. Row upon row of makeshift tents were lined up in neat orderly lines; it seemed the Egyptians spent a good deal of time and effort in making sure everybody had a good night's sleep which was important – it refreshes the body and mind, and a clear head was crucial and required by them all in the morning, where quick and decisive decision making could quite easily be the difference between a good day and a very bad day!

Three bundles of comfortable sheets made up their beds for the night. Tash took one end, Fluke in the middle with Baba gratefully taking the end bed.

'Are you nervous Tash?' asked Fluke, tucked up under his bed sheets, turning to Tash, waiting for an answer.

'Err, yeah of course!' She looked over at Fluke, 'Who wouldn't be nervous? You'd have to be superman not to feel a tiny bit scared. I mean, we're about to embark on a major historical battle Fluke, not some little squabble! How do you feel Baba?' They both rolled over to see what Baba had to say, but were greeted with a chorus of snoring, as Baba was already fast asleep.

'Lucky him!' yawned Tash, 'well, my left leg has just gone to sleep and I would like to catch it up! See you in the morning Fluke,' and she rolled over to get as much rest as she could, and within seconds Fluke had snoring in stereo – one side Tash, and the other side Baba, in competition with each other as to who could out-snore the other, and so far Tash was winning.

The rallying cry...

Fluke woke with a start. He'd been captured in the night by the Hittites and was bound from head to paw, tied securely so he couldn't escape. Desperate to free himself, he attempted to untangle himself from his tight restraints and make a run for it, but his paws were tied too tightly and he fell over, tripping over the end of Tash's bed and woke her with a start, when realisation dawned on him that it was just a dream.

'What on earth are you doing Fluke?' Tash looked over the edge of her bed sheets at her trusty companion, who was currently sat on the floor, bed sheets entwined around his legs and paws, with a sleepy and bewildered look on his face. It took Fluke several seconds to untangle himself from the ruffled up sheets.

'Sorry! I was dreaming again Tash, a bit too realistic for my liking, we'd been captured, tied up, tortured and...'

Tash laughed, 'I hope it's not a sign of things to come! Spending the rest of my life as a prisoner wasn't how I had mapped out my life! Don't worry Fluke, we've all got a lot on our mind. Still, you are useful for some things as you do make a great alarm clock! The sun must be due up in an hour or so, so we best get ready.'

They woke Baba from his deep slumber and Fluke and Tash changed into their battle costumes, whilst Baba made sure he had his trusty pens and parchment to make important notes in his diary. Addaya poked his head into the tent, glad to see they hadn't overslept, today of all days.

'C'mon, follow me you three. Ramesses is just about to give us all a speech, words of wisdom and last minute instructions.'

They followed Addaya out of the tent, and made their way over to where neat lines of Ramesses's battle hardened soldiers stood patiently, with the occasional murmur as troops talked in hushed voices to their closest colleagues, excitement and adrenalin coursing through their bodies as they waited for Ramesses to begin his speech.

Ramesses appeared at the top of a mound, and stood tall and proud surveying the scene spread out below him, the pride of his Egyptian army. The murmuring stopped and a hush fell over the expectant crowd.

'Friends...' Ramesses spoke with a powerful, but calming influence, his voice carried over the assembled crowd, 'we are all about to embark on an historic adventure – a mission to halt the

Hittite army and stop the threat they pose to the Egyptian Empire. We must stop their advance and send Muwatalli and his hordes back to their homeland, far away from the Egyptian borders. This is a mission to save and protect the good people of Egypt. Our lives and the lives of our families back home depend on the outcome. Today is a day that will live long in the memories, you will be talked about, honoured and treated as heroes. You all know what is expected of you, and although we are severely outnumbered I have the utmost faith that you will all carry out your duties and serve your country proudly.'

A huge roar swept through the crowd, everybody was pumped, eager and ready for the day's battle.

Ramesses paused and waited for the noise levels to drop, 'May the gods of Bastet and Anhur be with you at all times...' Ramesses gazed around, his eyes met Tash's and a smile spread over his face, 'now head off to your chariots and let battle commence!'

At the mention of Bastet, the cat goddess and goddess of war, heads turned and stared at Tash. They all thought with Bastet by their side there was no way they could lose, and inspired, they headed off to their waiting chariots.

Tash quickly entered the tent, retrieved their magic case, joined up with Fluke and Addaya and joined the waiting throng of charioteers. Just over 500 brand new two-man chariots all followed the lead chariot, with Ramesses at the head of the line, leading his Amun Division, heading out of camp to meet head on the advancing Hittites. It was an impressive sight, the chariots had been cleaned and polished; their occupants were armed with bows, arrows, spears and defensive shields.

Fluke hopped onto their magic case and sat behind Tash who adjusted the controls to manual mode, the case lifted several feet off the ground and hovered, remaining stationary. For once the case didn't spin round and shoot off at top speed, they didn't need the special time travel function, only needing the normal fly mode. The case joined the departing chariots, slowly making its way through the massed ranks, weaving in and out of the many chariots either side of them, until they reached the front, and fell in line just behind Ramesses and with Addaya at their side, forming an arrowhead formation, the chariots behind them spreading out.

'Where's Baba?' asked Fluke leaning over to talk to Addaya.

'On that mound behind us...' Addaya motioned with his thumb pointing over his shoulder, 'with some reserve chariots and a small back-up army of foot soldiers. His tactical notes will come in handy when we've finished today, Ramesses will want to see what improvements can be made for any future conflicts. You two stay close by my side, when Ramesses gives the word to charge it will be noisy, crazy and very scary!'

Into battle...

The sun was beginning to rise and peek over the horizon, but thankfully behind them, affording them a tactical advantage. Maybe with the sun in their eyes, the Hittites may be slightly blinded and hampered; any small advantage would be welcome.

Tash looked back to the front, and with her superb vision she spied a dark line on the horizon, getting steadily closer.

'I think we have company...' she muttered to Fluke, sat behind her, an arrow fixed in his bow string, with plenty of spare arrows close at hand.

'What, the Hittites?' he replied.

'I think so Fluke. That long line spread over the horizon is the Hittite chariots getting closer. I can just about make out their lead rider, it must be Muwattali.'

'So much for a surprise attack at dawn then: they must have had the same sneaky idea as us...' He grinned nervously, glancing over Tash's shoulder at the advancing enemy. 'There's thousands of them though, Tash, they have so many more chariots than us!'

'Have faith in Kahma's new chariots Fluke, they're fast, agile and also Addaya is the best military trainer and tactician in Egypt. His soldiers are the best of the best, and hopefully his Ptah and Seth Divisions aren't too far behind! His Re Division has re-grouped and are heading for the main Egyptian camp as back-up, so hopefully we won't be left stranded for too long.'

The gap between the two advancing armies was steadily closing. Ramesses stood tall and proud in the lead chariot, and turning around to face his soldiers, arm raised visibly in the air so all his following soldiers could clearly see. Waiting for the right moment he dropped his arm, the signal for his Amun Division to begin the charge.

The pace of the Egyptian advance quickened, a crescendo of noise from the horses, chariots and shouts of encouragement from his followers filled the air. They met head on the first wave of the approaching enemy. Ramesses fired the first arrow of the conflict, and a flurry of arrows followed, all being fired over Fluke and Tash's heads from the following archers. Ramesses reloaded another arrow and let fly again.

Fluke and Tash both stood on the case whilst maintaining their balance. The training they had received on the makeshift platform of a mock up chariot back in the city of Pi-Ramesses was proving advantageous, although it seemed a long time ago now, a distant memory.

Tash's first arrow found its intended target, the Hittite soldier falling from his chariot, causing the cumbersome three-man chariot to run out of control and overturn, spilling its two remaining occupants into the sand. Fluke followed suit and let fly, wounding his enemy from the slower chariot that was headed towards Ramesses.

'Their chariots are soooo slow compared to ours Tash...' Fluke beamed, 'they make an easy target to hit!'

The battle was raging all around, and a sea of arrows filled the air as the Hittites responded; their archers fired a volley of arrows towards the Egyptians, who responded by raising their shields over their heads, tilting them at an angle to provide a roof of protection. The arrows mainly bounced off the upturned shields and fell harmlessly into the sand.

The smile had been wiped off Fluke's face as he heard a series of dull thuds, and noticed with some considerable alarm their magic case had taken the brunt from a full volley of arrows, thankfully missing Tash, but sticking in the front of the case, adding more scars to their already battered case!

'That was close!' exclaimed Tash, ducking and thankfully missing another arrow. Looking all around she caught sight of Addaya and Ramesses, both had turned around in their chariots, and with arm signals instructed their following charioteers to spread out and try to come in from another angle and attack the Hittites from the side, rather than head on.

The Egyptians were heavily outnumbered, but tactically more astute than their opposition who relied heavily on a far greater number of soldiers. The fast and agile Egyptian chariots, at the predetermined hand signal commands given by Ramesses and Addaya, parted like the sea, letting the surprised Hittites advance straight down the middle. With the Egyptian chariots now on both of the outside flanks, their archers stood, and let fly a huge volley of arrows right into the heart of the Hittite ranks, causing confusion, panic and writing off several of the opposition chariots.

The magic case had weaved its way through the ranks of enemy chariots and flew straight through the rear lines of the Hittite chariots and into clear air. Slightly worse for wear, and with a few more scratches to add to its already battered appearance, the arrows sticking out the front of the case made it look like some giant porcupine.

As Tash was preparing to turn the case around to start another attack, she noted another line of approaching chariots: this must be a second wave of enemy. Ramesses had been outnumbered before, but this new wave of attackers stacked the odds even more heavily against the Egyptians.

Skill and tactical know-how was one thing, but eventually the far greater numbers would take its toll. Ramesses must be informed immediately, as he was probably unaware of the approaching enemy.

I have a plan...

Tash turned the magic case around 180 degrees and headed back into the melee. Upturned Hittite chariots were everywhere, and Tash steered carefully around them. Fluke was firing off arrows at whoever posed a threat and whenever the opportunity arose. They located Ramesses and Addaya: their magic case hovered back and forth, keeping pace with Ramesses's chariot.

'Muwatalli has a large contingent of reinforcements heading this way...' Tash said breathlessly, 'they're a short way off, not far behind the main Hittite lines and approaching fast,' she continued.

Ramesses rapidly pondered their predicament, turned to Addaya and asked, 'How far off are our Ptah and Seth Divisions?'

'A couple of hours would be my best guess,' confirmed Addaya.

'We must keep Muwatalli at bay until our reinforcements arrive,' Ramesses said through gritted teeth, firing off another salvo of arrows.

'I have an idea...' Tash said, ducking and manoeuvring their case as another arrow came whizzing close by, 'if you and your soldiers can contain this first wave of Hittites, me and Fluke will cause a distraction which will hopefully stall their advancing reinforcements long enough for our own back-up to arrive.'

Addaya looked at Ramesses, who shrugged. 'How?' Addaya voiced both their concerns.

Fluke agreed with Addaya and looked at Tash as if she had gone mad. 'You must have too much sand in your head,' he said shaking his head, 'the sand has replaced that normal sharp brain of yours, it's official folks...' he said sarcastically, 'Tash has finally lost the plot, you've gone bonkers Tash. The heat of the sun has affected what's left of your brain, stark raving mad! How are you...' he pointed at Tash with his paw, 'and me...' he jabbed his paw into his chest body armour, 'going to keep several hundred chariots at bay, on our own without help?'

Tash smiled back, and tapped her paw against the side of her nose, 'Oh trust me Fluke there's always a way. We just need to think clearly and use what we have at hand, and use it to our advantage. Look around, what do you see?'

Fluke gazed around, 'Apart from chariots, and there are lots of them I must add, there is sand, sand and lots more sand! Why...?' he added, slightly confused, 'Now's not a good time to be thinking about building sandcastles Tash.'

'Keep them occupied Addaya,' Tash grinned mischievously, 'we'll be back shortly to help mop up this lot!' She indicated with her paw the Hittites being picked off by Ramesses's Amun Division, and with a wave she turned their magic case around, and headed off in the direction of the approaching Hittite reinforcements.

'If you've got issues you want to talk about Tash, now would be a good time to air any problems you've got!' Fluke said, staring ahead at the approaching line of enemy chariots. 'We can discuss anything on your mind, if, or when we get home, there are experts you can talk to you know,' he said nervously.

'Have I ever let you down Fluke?' She turned to face Fluke. 'Do you trust me? I mean really trust me Fluke?' He looked her up and down, gave in, sighed, and said, 'Ok Tash, what's the plan?'

Once clear, they found themselves halfway between the ongoing battle and the line of approaching enemy. Stopping the case she hopped off and instructed Fluke to do the same.

'Oh great!' he said shaking his head, 'we're going to walk then are we? Great plan Tash. Let's just stroll up to that lot shall we...' he pointed towards the approaching enemy, 'and ask them to kindly go home as we're not ready for them?'

Tash ignored Fluke's comments, opened the case and rummaged around, deep inside the case's dark interior.

'Ah ha!' she exclaimed, pulling her paws out; she held two sets of swimming goggles.

Perplexed, Fluke looked at the goggles, then at Tash. 'Swimming goggles? For a start I can't swim, and secondly...' looking around 'I think the tide must be out, as I can't see much water around!'

'Put these on...' Tash instructed Fluke, 'and climb back on-board, we've got to hurry!' Doing as instructed, more to humour Tash than anything else, they both sat on the case. Tash continued, 'Right now wrap your headscarf around your face.'

'No armbands then?' Fluke was in full sarcasm mode now, wrapping his scarf securely around his face. 'I need armbands Tash if we're going swimming!'

'Right, now sling your bow over your shoulder, you're going to need two paws to hang on tight, and I mean very, very tightly!' Tash said.

'Why, are the waves going to cause us a problem? Is the water going to get a bit choppy?'

Fasset el 'afreet – the ghost wind...

'Right, are you hanging on?' Tash turned to Fluke, and chuckled at the sight of her companion wearing swimming goggles, his face fully covered by his headscarf. Fluke gave a muffled response which Tash assumed meant yes, and they headed off, the case rapidly picking up speed.

'Oh goody, the enemy!' said Fluke sarcastically, 'and we're armed with nothing more than swimming goggles! I can already see they're running away scared, we can't possibly lose!' Fluke's voice was barely audible through his headscarf.

Their magic case approached the advancing enemy, and rather than head straight into the centre, Tash steered sharply to the right, the case picking up speed, with Tash coaxing every bit of power from their case, 'C'mon, don't let us down now!' She patted the case with affection, their speed increasing by the second.

They went down the side of the Hittite chariots, around the back, and flew straight back up their left flank, eventually returning to the front where they had started. Their magic case circling the Hittite army was beginning to cause a major sandstorm: the quicker the case flew, the more sand was thrown up in the faces of the enemy. Tash kept the steering lock on, repeating the process, going round and round their enemy, rounding them up like a cattle herder.

The case continued its circular route completing several more circuits, getting faster and faster with each pass, causing havoc in the Hittite ranks. The front rank of chariot drivers were blinded and couldn't see a thing, causing chariots to crash into each other. The following chariots, not knowing what was happening, kept up the pace, and ploughed straight into the back of the chariots at the front who had stalled. Chaos and mayhem ensued, just what Tash had planned all along.

'I feel sick!' wailed Fluke, hanging on for dear life, grateful he was wearing goggles as the sand was everywhere. He was getting dizzier by the second, although he had to admit, tactically Tash had got it spot on – the confusion they were causing might just give them enough time for Ramesses's other Divisions to catch up.

Way off in the distance, Ramesses and Addaya, both wondering how Fluke and Tash were fairing, had re-grouped with their armoured Division, and just before they repeated another charge at their enemy, looked up. A huge smile was spread over Addaya's face as he witnessed the sandstorm in the distance.

'And they say I'm a master tactician...!' Turning to his Pharaoh Ramesses, he continued, 'I think we could learn a lot from Fluke and Tash – pure brilliance, utterly fantastic! I would never have thought about creating a *fasset el 'afreet,* look at the confusion in the opposing ranks, it's carnage, chariots crashing into each other, that should keep them tied up for a few hours!'

Tash decided she had had enough: she was getting dizzy herself, they'd created a diversion which should keep the Hittites occupied for a while, and she started to steer their magic case back towards Ramesses and Addaya.

Fancy a lift...

The battle between Ramesses and Muwatalli was almost at a stalemate, neither side appeared to be able to get the upper hand: the sides were evenly matched, until disaster struck. Ramesses's chariot was in the throes of battle with his Hittite counterpart, Muwattali, when his chariot caught something hidden in the sand and flipped over, tipping its driver and Ramesses out headfirst into the sand, his bow, shield and spear out of reach and out of sight as they became buried in the sand, completely hidden.

Muwattali, with an evil glint in his eye, sensed victory. He ordered his driver to turn their chariot around. Heading straight for the unarmed Ramesses, the Hittite leader's chariot bore down on the lonesome figure, who stood his ground, expecting the worse. Ramesses raised his head to the sky, closed his eyes, and prayed for some divine intervention.

Just as Muwattali was about to pass Ramesses and strike him down, out of nowhere the magic case flew past, with Fluke hollering at the top of his voice, 'Fancy a lift? Hop on board!' Ramesses opened his eyes, a smile spread over his face as he grabbed hold of Fluke's outstretched paw and gratefully leapt on board, sitting comfortably behind Fluke.

Fluke and Tash's flying chariot flew past a surprised looking Muwattali, who couldn't believe what he had just witnessed, his grin completely disappeared from his face as the chance to finish off his enemy was gone.

Tash handed Ramesses a spare bow and arrow set, which he gratefully accepted. He stood upright on the case, and side by side with Fluke they both fired off volley after volley of arrows.

The rest of Amun Division, buoyed by the sight of their rescued leader and safe in the knowledge that he had been saved by Fluke and Tash, had a renewed vigour; the feel-good factor spread through their ranks, which only intensified further when Addaya shouted at the top of his voice, 'Our reinforcements have arrived!'

Ramesses turned around, and glanced in the direction that Addaya had been pointing. Sure enough, closing rapidly were his Ptah and Seth Divisions, and also coming in from the side, and completely surprising Muwattali, were his Ne'arin troops. These new Egyptian arrivals evened up the numbers, causing panic in the Hittite ranks. Within minutes the tide of the battle had turned.

Muwattali looked around at his dishevelled army. His troops had a resigned look about them as one by one their chariots were turning around and fleeing back towards the safety of Kadesh. The Hittites were in full retreat, streaming back towards the Orontes River. Ramesses, sitting proudly behind Tash on the magic case, urged his men to give chase. In desperation, the Hittites that reached the river abandoned their chariots and faced the ultimate humiliation of having to swim across, much to the delight of the Egyptians.

Ramesses stood on the river bank, abandoned chariots littering the sandy floor. His men cheered and mocked the retreating army as they swam back to relative safety. Amongst the swimmers was Muwatalli, who dragged himself up the far river bank, dripping wet; he turned, and stared back across the river, the two old foes eyed each other up and down. Deep down, they both knew this was a battle neither side could convincingly win – two great armies matching each other. The look they gave each other was of a begrudging respect, and they both knew a draw was the only real conclusion. The Egyptians had failed in their attempt to take the town of Kadesh, but equally the Hittites' advance towards Egypt had failed, their quest to take control of Egypt was scuppered.

Muwatalli turned around, and ordered the retreat of his army, they were heading home, back to the Hittite heartland.

Return to base camp...

Fluke, Tash and Ramesses rode back to camp on the magic case and met up with a relived looking Baba who ran towards the pair, glad that they had returned relatively unscathed, although he noticed their case had taken a bit of a battering, arrows were embedded in the front, sides and back.

'You're safe...' exclaimed Baba, 'I was watching the battle unfold from the high ground, right here.' He pointed to a raised plateau. 'What you did to create the *fasset el 'afreet* was remarkable.'

Addaya came over, and agreed with young Baba. 'Spectacular tactics! If it hadn't been for you two and the magic case, we could have been in a whole heap of trouble. Ramesses will be eternally grateful of that you can be sure.'

They all hushed as Ramesses climbed off the case and approached Fluke and Tash. 'Thank you both for saving my life. I prayed to the gods for help and they sent me Bastet – the cat goddess riding in on a magical flying chariot to whisk me away seconds before Muwatalli could get to me. Not only did you save my life, but you also helped save the Egyptian people, the battle turned in our favour from that moment on, and Muwatalli has been sent home, and I don't think he will return anytime soon! We cannot claim a complete victory...' he said turning to his men, 'but we can certainly claim a moral victory if nothing else!'

The next three to four days were spent counting the cost of the war. Casualties were treated, damaged chariots were fixed and a roll call was taken to identity any missing soldiers; thankfully that particular list was very short. It had been decided to pack up and start the long march back home to Pi-Ramesses. Everyone had been through so much and seen enough of the war. They all wanted to leave Kadesh, each and every soldier, regardless of rank, wished to head home and be back with their family.

Tash had agreed to make several journeys back and forth playing taxi; firstly she took Baba, and over the next three days several more trips were made ferrying some of Ramesses's top generals.

Addaya had flatly refused the first few rides back home. He wanted to oversee the dismantling of their huge camp, making sure everything was ready for the month-long march home.

As the last chariot disappeared from view, Ramesses stood alongside his faithful friend Addaya, and new-found colleague Fluke, all three waiting patiently for the return of Tash on the magic case.

A small sandstorm was fast approaching. Fluke, realising who it was, pulled down his swimming goggles to prevent any sand getting into his eyes. Tash skidded to a halt right in front of them, throwing up a load of sand, covering them from head to toe, or in Fluke's case head to paw.

Tash looked around and said, 'That's that then? The camp has been cleared and everybody has started to make the long march home. Hop on board and let's get going, firstly back to Pi-Ramesses and then we've got to get Baba back home to Deir-el-Medina; his mum and dad will be worried about him.'

'Yeah, back to Deir-el-Medina! I hope Abana has been baking bread, she's a wonderful cook.' Fluke was virtually drooling at the prospect of one of Abana's home cooked dinners.

'You and your appetite Fluke...' laughed Tash, 'we've just been in the largest chariot battle in history and you're thinking about your stomach again.'

'Well there's an old saying...' he replied with a smile, 'an army marches on its stomach, and let's face it we've all done a heck of a lot of marching just recently, so hurry up and get us all home. I can smell Abana's cooking from here!' he joked, and everybody joined in the good natured banter.

Welcome home party...

They arrived back at Pi-Ramesses to a hero's welcome. The people of the city thronged the main square, waiting in anticipation for the safe return of their great Pharaoh. The flying chariot was famous, Baba had been back for three days now, spreading the word about their escapades, telling everybody present as to how the battle of Kadesh unfolded. How Bastet and her faithful companion Fluke, had rescued Ramesses. A small celebration was planned for that night – Pi-Ramesses was going to be the party capital of Egypt; its citizens were determined to celebrate the safe return of their beloved Pharaoh.

A gasp rippled around the expectant crowd as they all looked to the heavens to witness the arrival of the flying chariot. For once Tash executed a perfect landing, right in the centre of the main square. Ramesses's wife and children stood alongside his generals, aides and other dignitaries, Khama was there as well to greet the returning heroes. They all rushed over to the suitcase: each and every person wanted to be the first to pass on their congratulations.

Fluke and Tash were formerly introduced to Nefertari, Ramesses's wife. They also met his siblings, Amunherkhepeshef, the eldest Crown Prince and Commander of the Troops, and Pareherwenemef, who, when he was a bit older, would serve alongside his elder brother and join Ramesses's army in future campaigns.

They were escorted to the main residential palace, a truly grand structure fronted by a huge lake and surrounded by many canals, which Tash thought had an uncanny resemblance to modern day Venice.

They were given a guided tour of the grand palace and were shown to their rooms to freshen up.

'What a beautiful palace!' Fluke exclaimed when Nefertari left the room, heading off to help organise that night's party.

'Not bad is it!' Tash wholeheartedly agreed, opening the magic case and throwing in her dirty clothes. Quite how the magic case worked she didn't know, but within seconds it had churned out a fresh and clean set, neatly pressed and smelling divine.

Fluke did the same with his old clothing, glad to be rid of the smelly old clothes he had been wearing for several days now and they both changed quickly, ready for the evening's entertainment.

The party was in full swing when they arrived back in the main square. Food and music were plentiful, people from of all walks of life mixed with each other, the royal family were circulating and chatting to everyone. Some of the generals Tash had brought back were trading stories from their experiences at the battle of Kadesh. This party was just a warm up celebration for when all of Ramesses's army returned in full, but as that wouldn't be for another month, tonight's bash was an excuse to let their hair down, it was obvious to see that the Egyptians loved to celebrate!

Deir-el-Medina...

The party went on into the early hours, and when Fluke and Tash eventually woke several hours later it was mid-morning. Everything had been cleaned away, the main square was spotless, and you wouldn't have guessed that any celebration had taken place; life at Pi-Ramesses appeared to be back to normal.

'We better think about getting you home, Baba,' Tash stretched and yawned. 'Your mum and dad will be missing you – it's been several days since we left.'

'No need to worry about that. I sent Dad a message three days ago letting him know we were all ok and explained how the battle went. I also told Dad that Khama's new chariot design was a success and that he will be coming back with us.'

'Message?' Fluke queried, joining in the conversation, 'I didn't know you had a mobile phone?'

'Mobile phones?' said a confused Baba, 'what are they? Anyway...' Baba continued, giving Fluke a sideways glance, 'I sent a message with some of our carrier pigeons. I might have mentioned the part you two played as well, so there may be a surprise waiting for you when we get home!'

They packed up their belongings, Baba made sure he had all his notes, pens and parchment paper, and they all went off in search of Khama. It was time to head back.

Khama was in the throes of saying his farewells to Addaya and Ramesses, who had given all his workers some extended holiday; he figured it was the least a kind and caring Pharaoh could offer to his trusty staff.

Ramesses and Addaya turned to embrace Fluke and Tash with a hearty round of handshakes and plenty of hugs.

'Have a safe trip home,' Addaya said, 'and once again thank you both. You and your flying chariot will long be remembered by us all.'

Fluke, Tash, Baba and Khama mounted the magic case. Tash double checked her co-ordinates, turned the handle three times which engaged the gears, and with a final wave goodbye the case spun a few times and promptly disappeared from sight, leaving a bewildered looking Ramesses and Addaya staring at the empty spot where the case had been only seconds ago.

The return journey to Deir-el-Medina was quick, and in a matter of seconds they were flying over the village. Baba looked down, his fear of heights was nowhere near as much as Fluke's, who still occasionally flew with his eyes shut.

'Mum, Dad – up here!' he hollered and waved as they passed over his house. Salatis and Abana were outside looking up, Baba's letter had indicated an approximate time that they would be returning, and his parents witnessed the case coming into a near perfect landing. The main street was long and straight, so it made a natural runway. The case had banked around and flew down the centre of the high street, skidding to a halt right outside Baba's front door.

'Welcome home Son.' Baba's mother and father eagerly embraced him, practically dragging him off the magic case, such was their enthusiasm to make sure their son was still in one piece.

'Kahma, my old friend...' said Salatis approaching Kahma who had just stepped down from the case, 'I'm so glad you're ok. Reading Baba's letter he sent us via carrier pigeon, it certainly sounds like it was an eventful few days for everyone, and the Hittites have been sent packing, and Egypt is safe for the time being.'

'Through the skills and courage of these two,' Kahma indicated Fluke and Tash. 'They rescued Ramesses in his hour of need, without them, the outcome of the battle would have been totally different.'

Salatis walked over and shook paws with Fluke and Tash, 'I hear you two are now heroes, Baba told us everything in his letter. You must know by now he's very thorough, and goes into great detail, the whole village is talking about what you've achieved.'

'We only played a small part in the battle...' said Tash. 'We only did what anybody would have done in our position,' Tash continued rather sheepishly. Taking praise didn't come naturally for either of them.

'Well, tonight we shall have a small family get together,' Abana said.

'Have you been baking, Mum?' Baba asked eagerly, 'it's just Fluke has been asking and wanted to know if you had been making your famous bread! He says he's been looking forward to sampling it one more time before they head off home.'

'Yes Son,' she smiled, 'I've been baking especially for you all. Nedjem and her mother are popping over shortly. Nedjem is so eager to see you again, apparently she's missed you!'

'And no rushing off tomorrow either,' said Salatis pointing to Fluke and Tash, 'we have a surprise to show you. Something we hope will honour the pair of you.'

'Now I'm confused,' said Fluke, scratching an itchy spot behind his ear, looking at Tash for an explanation.

'Don't look at me,' she shrugged and replied, 'I don't know what they've got up their sleeves. I guess we'll find out tomorrow.'

Pyramidion...

The family get-together went smoothly and the promised feast was plentiful. Fluke had his fill of Abana's home baking, devouring every last morsel that was placed before him. Nedjem and her mother arrived; Baba was so excited to see his girlfriend again, that he never left her side all evening until eventually Nedjem's mother called an end to the evening and headed home.

Tash woke early the next morning to be greeted by bright sunlight streaming through the open window.

'Come on sleepy...' she said, prodding the loose bundle of bedding next to her, eager to wake Fluke, 'we've got a big day today, it's our last day in Egypt and we can't waste it by snoozing all day.'

'What are you doing?' said a voice behind her.

'Trying to wake Fluke, he's overslept again...' her voice trailed off and she spun around, suddenly recognising the voice.

Fluke entered the bedroom and stared down at the bedding that Tash had been prodding. 'I think you'll find for once it's *you* that has overslept and not me...' he laughed. 'I've been up ages, had breakfast and been for an early morning walk down to the river bank.'

Abana entered the spare room and confirmed that Fluke had indeed been up and out for a walk. 'He's even helped clean up last night's dishes,' she smiled and ruffled Fluke's head.

Bemused at the prospect of Fluke actually getting up before her, *and* that he'd actually helped clean up, left Tash muttering to herself as she helped Abana fold up their bedding.

Their case was packed and stored in the kitchen just waiting to head home when Fluke remembered last night's conversation. 'So what's the surprise you have in store for us?' he asked as he turned to Salatis for an answer.

'We'll have to show you rather than tell you.' Salatis grinned and turning to Baba continued, 'Are you ready, Son?'

'Of course Dad,' Baba confirmed his readiness and the whole family headed out of the door.

'To the Valley of the Kings then!' said Salatis marching off, closely followed by Abana, Baba and Fluke, with Tash bringing up the rear struggling with the case.

'I thought I was Bastet the royal cat goddess!' she laughed, 'so why have I got to carry the case?'

'Well, to me you're just plain old *Tash,* the family cat...' Fluke replied, 'and it's your turn, remember? I carried it here and you're carrying it back.'

The group approached the Valley of the Kings, and Salatis steered Fluke and Tash over to the main pyramid that they had helped build and decorate several days ago.

'Well, if it's not my two young apprentices returning to witness the finishing touches to the great pyramid.'

Tash looked around to locate the owner of the voice, 'Ishpi! How are you?' Ishpi continued over to stand between Fluke and Tash and put his arms around the pair and carried on, 'Today is a special day, the day the pyramid is finally finished.'

'What happens now then?' queried Tash.

'It's when we put the final capstone in place, right at the top. We call it Benbenet or Pyramidion and cover it in gold leaf. The sun's rays reflect off the gold, so it's quite a spectacular sight.' Sure enough, as the Pyramidion was slipped into place, by none other than Maya and Hapu, the two friendly Nummers and head stonemasons, the sun shone brightly and its rays reflected off the gold leaf, drawing gasps of awe from the assembled crowd.

'Spectacular...' gasped Fluke, staring up in awe at the towering pyramid, bedecked with its new gold top. Turning to an equally impressed Tash he continued, 'Truly stunning. I still find it hard to believe the Egyptians manage to build something so huge, and so accurately without using modern tools and equipment. I think even our modern day builders would struggle to get it looking as good.'

Salatis interrupted Fluke's thoughts, 'One more surprise for you both. If you two would follow Ishpi, he has someone that wants to meet you again.'

Fluke, Tash, Salatis and Baba all followed Ishpi into the pyramid itself. They headed ever deeper into the bowels of the pyramid, and eventually came into the main burial chamber, and there to greet them was Nebitka, the master painter.

'Welcome back...' grinned Nebitka, who was a kindly man and had taken a shine to the pair. 'We've all heard about your escapades and adventures in the battle of Kadesh, and thought it was fitting that we paint a permanent reminder of your adventure.' Nebitka stepped aside to allow Fluke and Tash an uninterrupted view of the large wall that was now adorned with a huge painting.

'Will you look at that?' exclaimed Tash, and for once even Fluke was near speechless. The painting was an accurate portrayal of the whole battle scene, and there, in pride of place, were Fluke and Tash riding on their flying chariot. The first scene showed them riding alongside Ramesses heading into battle; the second scene showed how the flying chariot had caused the fasset el 'afreet; and finally, the third scene was when they had rescued Ramesses in his hour of need.

'We're famous Tash,' beamed Fluke, a large grin spread over his face.

'I think we're just glad that we could help in some way...' Tash said turning around to their new friends, 'and we're certainly going to miss the excitement around here.'

Ancient Greece adventure...

Fluke and Tash left the depths of the burial chamber taking a long slow walk back up to the surface, neither really wanting to go home so soon. They had made some great friends along the way, and had been in what can only be described as an exciting adventure. Reaching the surface they both took a last long lingering look around. The great Ramesses pyramid that they had helped build stood towering in its majestic glory, now fully complete with its gold Pyramidion gleaming brightly, its golden rays reaching far and wide.

They both got emotional as one by one their friends filtered by, some shaking their paws, but most giving the pair big hugs. Last in line was Baba, with a sad look on his face.

'I'm really going to miss you both...' he said sniffing and wiping away a tear that had appeared and was rolling slowly down his cheek, 'it's been the best few days of my life – who would have thought a few days ago the adventures we would have got up to! Do you really have to go? I mean you know you can stay, can't they Dad?'

'They've got to go Son, they have their own lives to lead, but they will both be welcomed back any time.' Turning to Fluke and Tash, Salatis continued, 'You have an open invitation which applies to special guests, our house is your house, and Son...' he said turning to Baba, 'you can't ever forget them, their painting is a permanent reminder, you've only got to come here and see it whenever you want.'

'You take care Baba...' Tash said, 'with a teacher like your dad, you've got a great future ahead of you, and look after Nedjem as she's one in a million!'

'We'll read all about your work in the history books when we get home Baba, of that I can promise,' confirmed Fluke.

With a sigh, they mounted their flying chariot. Tash set the co-ordinates, and with both waving goodbye for the final time, she turned the handle three times causing the case to spin, and promptly disappeared in a mini sandstorm.

Baba strode over to the now empty space recently vacated by the case, staring into the distance. His dad put a consoling arm around his son as they walked off with Abana and headed home.

The magic case made a dramatic entry back home, just missing the ironing board by inches, and skidded through the bedroom door and nestled up against the wardrobe door.

'Shhh!' whispered Tash, climbing gingerly off the case. Fluke looked over at the illuminated digital clock which showed the time of 12:24.

'We've only been gone two minutes Tash...' said Fluke, 'but it really seems like we've been gone weeks. Oh, but what a great adventure we've just had!' He grinned as they quietly packed away their clothes, putting them neatly back into the case. Tash opened the wardrobe door and carefully stored their magic case inside, tucked away and hidden behind old jackets and clothes that hadn't been worn in ages.

'So where to next?' Fluke whispered to Tash as they crept along the landing to their bedroom.

Climbing up onto the sofa and curling up, Tash yawned and said, 'Don't know Fluke, but wherever we go, Egypt will take some beating.' And with heavy eyelids she was asleep in seconds.

'How about ancient Greece? They have some amazing history to discover Tash. The Olympic Games originated there, temples like the Parthenon, ancient gods such as Apollo, Poseidon and Zeus, mythical monsters like the Minotaur and...' Fluke stopped his whispering as he noticed Tash was fast asleep and hadn't heard a word he'd said.

'Other monsters and gods,' he continued talking to himself, 'I hope they don't have a cat goddess,' he chuckled, 'they might even have a dog god, and it can be *my* turn to be worshiped for a change!'

Contented and comfy, Fluke joined Tash in a snoring competition and drifted off into a deep sleep, dreaming of their next exciting adventure.